TAHOMA
LITERARY
REVIEW

tahomaliteraryreview.com

TAHOMA LITERARY REVIEW
Number 19
Fall/Winter 2020
ISBN-13: 978-1-7331052-8-6

Copyright © 2020 Tahoma Literary Review
Washington • California

tahomaliteraryreview.com

Tahoma Literary Review

About the Cover

"Truth of Peace and Arrows," Raul Pizarro

"Truth of Peace and Arrows" was one of my first bear paintings, most of which were created during my nephew's early years. He was nonverbal the first three years of his life. Every morning he would come over and wait for me on a little bench in front of my house, eager for me to draw for him. In an attempt to help him start speaking, I would ask him what he wanted me to doodle. His requests were usually bears going noni (sleeping) or elephants reading books.

I asked what the bear should be doing in each sketch, and with every question my nephew's one word became two, then three, slowly morphing into full sentences. As he started to flourish, a new awakening inside of me did too. His voice bloomed and so did mine. The bears I had been creating were challenging my own beliefs about life. I realized how much of my life I had been an observer, not fully present.

This painting is based on those moments with my nephew, moments that revealed a broader spectrum of existence, one that encompasses joy, fear, and enlightenment.

I am a visual artist with muscular dystrophy. I was born in Mexicali, Mexico, the third of four siblings. We migrated to Southern California—the place that reared me and became home after the age of three.

My work bridges diverse themes and spans over twenty-five years; each piece of art emerged from an experience at the intersection of disability, LGBTQ identity, race and ethnicity, family and community. Find me and my work at RaulPizarro.com.

My residency with Self-Help Graphics in Los Angeles is one of my proudest achievements. Working with a master printmaker, we produced several prints of "Sharia," and half became part of various Latinx collections at museums and universities nationally. I was also one of the artists invited to participate in the singular Los Angeles' Community of Angels project, and this year, was featured in "Preserving Creative Spaces," a traveling collection of fifty photographs of artists and their studios that will become part of the Smithsonian archives.

TABLE OF CONTENTS

You can hear many of the authors in this issue read their stories, poems, and essays at https://soundcloud.com/tahomaliterary/tracks

ABOUT THIS ISSUE

Transitions were on my mind while we put this issue together. Big and small, personal and global, dramatic changes filled the four months it took to produce the latest issue of *Tahoma Literary Review*. On the smaller scale, our magazine staff faced a period of staff turnover. While few in absolute numbers (two left, three joined, one changed positions), for *TLR* it meant that almost half of the names on the masthead changed.

More broadly, what needs to be said about events in the wider world? A pandemic that infected millions; protests that proclaimed Black Lives Matter; natural disasters that climate change exacerbated . . . we have experienced transitions of epic proportions. And as this issue goes to print, we are poised for another potentially tumultuous change: the Presidential election.

Transitions are to some degree inevitable, and when they happen, they are inevitably disruptive. The pandemic, the protests, climate change, the election are all forcing change on us. Some of those changes may be hard, they may test our resilience, and our responses matter. They demonstrate who we are. We can admire—and choose to be among—those who use such moments to create something better.

The events that have surrounded us reminded me how fundamental transitions are in writing. Change is movement; it brings tension. A character's growth can mark the difference between a short story and an anecdote; personal revelations elevate pithy observations into an essay; and the incisive transformation of an image into a broader metaphor creates a poem. True to this idea, at least one transition dwells in each of this issue's selections. In a short story it can be a character's new perspective about their childhood. In an essay it is an insight into the legacy of one's own heritage. In a poem it is a daughter's impulsive gesture. This motion, these steps forward, change something within the work, and may change something in the reader, too.

We hope you enjoy the works we've selected for this issue. Visit us online and let us know what you think on Facebook, Instagram, or Twitter.

Twitter (@tahomareview)
Instagram (@tahomareview)
Facebook (facebook.com/TahomaLiteraryReview)
SoundCloud (soundcloud.com/tahomaliterary)

TAHOMA
LITERARY
REVIEW

MIDDLE SCHOOL
DEREK SHEFFIELD

She throws open the door and hops out
with backpack and clarinet, then turns
to walk away as her glance
takes in her classmates

passing through the front doors,
bending to lock their bikes,
standing in small groups,
and in her face something happens,

she's someone else
who plucks off her pink headband
with its pink bow dotted with hearts,
checks to see if anyone saw,

and quickly hands it to me.
All last year and the years before,
since her first wisps of hair,
headbands have marked her

with colors, weeks going by
bright as wildflowers. Now a sideways look,
a brief lift of her hand, and bareheaded
she walks toward the school.

I watch every step I can, holding
the headband with the bow,
a pink U, a horseshoe. Not
for luck, I know, but letting go.

BRODY'S LETTER

BY SANDY BRIAN HAGER

Whenwewerekidsmycousin Brody delivered an envelope to my dad on em orningbeforeschool. Yearslater I learnedthatitcontainedatypewrittenlett erwherein Brodyexpressedhisgratitudetomydad for actinglike a dad becau se Brody'sowndadhadlefthismom when shewasstillpregnantwithhim. I re callcatchingaglimpseoftheenvelope'scontentsbeforedadlefttheroom to r eaditinprivacy. The child's enchanted world! I thought Brody managed to cr eatehisowncrosswordpuzzle, when infact the just didn't know how to use the spacebar.

Your Subscription Is Expiring

Jinwoo Chong

On the day that The Title shutters, I observe: number one, that magazines tend to die very much like the sickly plants of negligent people, leaves yellowing in full view until they are thrown into the garbage, upon which it is clear that their abject failure to be has been assured for years; and number two, that my father, whom I had disappointed by choosing a career in print media, had been right all along, a fact he might relish if still alive. Given that my observations—along with my job—are now valueless, I remain silent as my supervisor. With a progress bar on his monitor estimating the completed deletion of our office server, he tells me that there will be no severance pay and to vacate the building within the hour.

"This *does* remind me," my supervisor says. He had come to the office in sneakers and a pair of running shorts that exposed spiderweb veins on his white, hairless legs. "Would you be a reference? It's this sperm startup. They say they're looking for somebody to head up partnerships. I reached out after the Lunar New Year giveaway. They absolutely loved our messaging."

"What is a sperm startup?" I ask. I ignore the fact that the Lunar New Year giveaway (decorative tote bag and raffle entry with paid subscription renewal) was not only my project but one that ran two months ago, before The Title's publisher had even declared bankruptcy.

"Something to do with icing your little guys until you and the missus are baby-ready. Did you know fertility in men is plummeting? How come nobody's talking about that?"

The window is open, we sweat through our shirts in the middle of summer. My supervisor is a year younger than me; we are the last two of a team that had once been twenty. Together we have watched The Title's print schedule shrink over the years, first weekly, then bi-weekly, and monthly since last year, gutted to its bare bones after employees at our Tampa fulfillment center threatened a mass exit over dwindling pay. Ours was one of several prestige brands hung out to dry as revenues tanked. We had even failed to attract the interest of an ambitious and benevolent billionaire, many a magazine's last hope these days. A sports title sold off two years ago had named its new owner's grandson a Pick to Watch in the upcoming draft. He signed with the Bengals, my supervisor told me one day. I didn't know which sport that was.

My supervisor steals glances at me while stacking his hoarded gym shoes on the edge of his desk. I remember that he has asked me a question and supply my personal email. He doesn't have anything more to say to me.

This is the future my father feared; I was diligent, punctual, I performed my duties with integrity but had no other skills that rendered me of any attraction to employers. There had been no moves to take The Title digital in the last decade; research had found a high probability that it would alienate our readership, an equal parity of men and women over thirty-five, high-net-worth heads of families, eighty-three percent of whom still renewed their subscriptions by paper mail. I will find another magazine, I think to myself, a smaller title of flickering dignity, at a decreased salary. I would stay there, writing off little slips of cardstock stamped with Alert! Alert! Your Subscription Is Expiring! until it too shuttered, and I'd find myself in a similar room, with a similar supervisor, again with no benefits, with no severance check.

Again thinking of my father, his heavy face and his coldness, the things I remembered most clearly following his separation from my mother shortly before Christmas those years ago, an inkblot that had devoured what I recalled of his kindness—and there had been kindness—after my mother left. I do think he feared for me, there was at least a small portion of the man that felt unease rather than disappointment at my choices. After all, he had stayed, he had raised me after my mother had left us in the little house, and its manicured trees in rows: living remnants of our once-perfection.

I stand, and my back is soaked through with sweat, I move through the heat as though wading in water. Three pristine copies of The Title's final print issue lay on the chair by the door, and I stop to look at them.

"What are those doing here?" I ask.

My supervisor glances my way, then at the copies, snorts.

"Tampa sent those to us. Get this. There's one guy left in the Legacy subscription bracket. One guy! The system already emptied out the segment so there was no way to mail it. I told them what the fuck, they just laughed at me over the phone and hung up—"

I pick up the three copies, on the cover a glossy profile of a former First Lady that might have been published today or five years ago. There is no notice, no mention of the shuttering in the editor's letter on the first page. The end of a century-old institution. The address box in the bottom-left corner is blank. It doesn't surprise me that the Legacy bracket, subscribers renewed at least 5 times in the past 10 years, ranked highest in loyalty, is defunct. The price point (a dollar more than the single issues sold at newsstands) was, in my words, a scam.

"One guy, huh."

"I could let the intern deliver it by hand," my supervisor says, "give that kid one last fuck you. That always feels good."

"You mean this person lives here? In the city?"

My supervisor blinks at me. He digs around his table, snatching up a post-it with an address written on it. He hands it to me with a shrug. We have worked together for ten years. He is an only child. He took jogs before his lunch breaks and changed awkwardly behind his desk afterwards. Grew up out of state. I can't think of anything else.

"Poetic," he says. "One last guy gets his magazine the old-fashioned way. Almost makes you proud, doesn't it?" The smell of his stacked running shoes is beginning to nauseate me. My watch reads quarter past noon.

"Yeah," I say, my final words to him.

I step outside, into dust carried high and hot by the wind. I blink, crying tears, and glance at the address I've been given. I know the neighborhood, conveniently bypassed by the major bus lines. I fold the note twice and tuck it into my pocket. I slide the issues between two manila folders in my backpack, taking care not to stub any corners. One for the subscriber. I might keep the other two. If the publisher had no interest in archiving them, at the very least I would. I walk.

Behind me, my office building looms, home to the American headquarters of a German bank, an ultra-luxe gym, and an array of high-to-low retail in the lobby. I nudge shoulders down the baking sidewalk. I have enjoyed this area of the neighborhood, attracting throngs to the cobbled streets (some of the oldest in the city) and evacuating conveniently before sundown. At this hour of the day, stragglers remain, cyclists and speed walkers with free reign of the streets. I walk a mile or so, wiping my forehead dry with my grimy hands. I have given much thought to this moment in the forty-eight hours since news of The Title's discontinuation was delivered to me by email. No job, no health insurance, not a next step in sight. And yet, what I had envisioned to be frightful and vast is instead a deep calm. I observe: that I embark on this mission willingly, that there is nothing to stop me taking the magazines home for myself, or, better yet, throwing them in the nearest garbage can and going home, perhaps to start revising my resume. I reach another mile, checking the distance on my phone, and come to that handy realization: that I am too far gone, that I, a lover of order and utility, must make use of this wasted time. My last subscriber is waiting for his issue.

My father had once received The Title at our home. I recalled its weekly arrival from a young age. I'd pass it hanging over the edge of our coffee table, half-read. He used it as a prop, the way most magazines are, being that it mattered less what was in them and more that a guest of the house could spot a stack of them by the television remote and know this was an intelligent house, my father's magazines, my mother's carefully pruned trees in their neat rows in the front yard. If my father ever read them, cover-to-cover, I would never know. He was far too busy for it, I suspect, travelling often for work. When he was home, he preferred to interview my mother and I over dinner, absorbing the events of our day and offering his advice on any complications and dilemmas without solicitation. This, too, changed, after my mother left home and the two of us behind, his occasional punctuations of our daily silence would be equal parts shocking and brief. I did not think such a person existed, a man with the ability to settle into a sameness that to others looked as worn and routine as time and to me resembled that of a stranger.

"Hey—"

Somebody shouts, off to my right, and the sound jars me from my thoughts. A ratty teenager fights his way through a current of tourists to reach me and loses his balance, falling roughly into my arms. I am inundated with the smell of cigarette smoke. He backs off, embarrassed, squinting at me.

"You are..." he begins, "not the person I thought you were."

"I'm sorry?"

"No, I'm sorry," he says, gathering himself up, a knobby sweater that hangs off his shoulders and exposes a bare stretch of his skin. "I thought you were somebody else. Sorry."

He leaves me there, casting a wide berth around a family whose mother herds her children away from him, and sits back down on the stone steps of a bank building. At his feet is a beaten rucksack. He is an insect on the pristine surface of the grey marble. The doormen would call the police soon, I think, if he stayed any longer. I cross the sidewalk over to him.

"Who did I look like?"

"Friend's dad," he shrugs, squinting up at me.

"You always run after people you think you recognize?"

He gestures to the steps around him. "Do I look like I have something better to do?"

A brisk wind rips through the street and he hugs himself close, breathing into his grubby hands. A suited man approaches the glass doors behind us. He wags a delicate finger at me, slowly, like a metronome at waltz-tempo.

"Have you eaten?"

The kid laughs, though I catch just before the glaze of his manufactured ease covers his face a flash of pleasant surprise.

"Why?"

I turn what I'm about to say over in my head, looking for faults.

"I'd like to know if you're hungry, and if I might buy you some dinner."

He does not think about it very hard, springing to his feet with his rucksack. He gestures with a wave of his arm, and I lead him down the sidewalk. He kicks the fallen orange leaves in his path. The taller buildings melt away, swallowed up by the sun as more and more of it, the noise, the clogged air, dissipates around us. I observe: a diner on the corner of the next block. We cross the street. I follow him inside. He slides into a booth by the windows, warming his hands.

"Whatever you want," I tell him. A burger, a milkshake, two slices of reheated pizza and a cup of soup arrive after ten minutes of our non-conversation, and he wolfs it all and I think about how there is little hunger like his in my life, for anything.

"What are you doing here?"

"Is that a serious question?" he asks me, wiping his mouth.

I try again, wanting to please him. "What you brought you to those stairs?"

He looks at me, patiently, and I worry I've gone too far.

"Flunked too many classes, stole too much money. In my defense, I was seeing a guy, I was distracted. Not sure it convinced my dad."

"Do your parents know where you are?"

He shrugs. "School started a month ago. If they wanted me back they would've come and found me." The way he breaks his gaze indicates he doesn't want to talk about it anymore. I can think of no advice. He eats until he's full, refusing my offer to bag something for him to go, something hot to keep his hands warm.

"Look at you," he says, "Nice clothes, nice hair. You must have some cunt-y job in one of those big glass buildings."

"I was laid off today."

He makes a hiss between his teeth, a gesture of pain.

"Sure you want to spend all this money on me?"

I shrug. He gazes at me with apathy, or perhaps only non-judgment. I've never been able to tell. I remove the issues from my bag and explain my mission. He reaches for the topmost before I can stop him, smearing a corner with ketchup.

"Oh—shit."

"It's . . . okay," I force myself to say. It is all it takes; I have no power to be angry with this boy. I would keep only one, then. Easier. I could have it framed, if I wished. "You take that one if you like."

He shrugs, folding it in half and crushing it within a pocket of his rucksack. "You're kind. Your mom and dad must love you."

"They're dead."

"Both?"

"My father is. I haven't seen my mother in twenty-two years."

"Divorced?"

"They were never married, actually. Didn't believe in it."

He makes an 'o' with his lips, genuinely concerned, and I am surprised at his thoughtfulness. "They break our hearts, don't they," he says, appearing even as he says it to shrink away from its uselessness, its honeyed-ness. "And we break theirs."

Something true in there, I suppose. Maybe I am trying to comfort him, in supposing. I still miss my mother. I do not wonder any more why she never came back, having exhausted so much of my teens asking the same question of my father, whose non-answers only hardened me further. After my mother left, the trees in the yard, her pride and joy, grew wild and unkempt along with us. Soon, I did not care.

He finishes his food, leaning away from the empty plates. "So where are we going?"

"What?"

"Your place? Hotel?" he swivels his neck, looking around the nearly empty diner. "Bathroom?"

"What? No—" I stammer, "I didn't mean—that's not what I want."

He frowns, not understanding. He picks up the long spoon his milkshake came with and dips it for the dregs, as though I might swipe it all off the table in a rage.

"You know, I didn't really peg you for discreet, the way you just walked up and asked—"

"I don't want any of that. You just looked hungry."

He dawdles, as if weighing my words, picking at something on his fingernail. He raises his head and I see for the first time a clearness. He really was so young. He reaches forward and takes my face in both of his hands, a strange gesture. Within them I feel his power, he is better at this than me. We pass one more moment like this, with his hands on me. Then he stands up, taking his bag with him. He hitches it over his shoulder. He digs in his back pocket for something and places it, gently, on the table between us. I peer at it, confused, until I recognize its frayed stitching: my wallet. He smiles, sheepishly at me.

"You were too easy," he says. "But you made me feel bad."

"My luck," I smile.

He nods, walks past me, out the door. I pay for his meal, finding all my cards and bills intact, and see myself outside. The sky is dark overhead, the sun having dipped below sometime while we ate. A breeze wafts its way between my legs and under my arms.

With time on my hands, I begin to imagine that recipient of my efforts, the Legacy subscriber for whom I'd come this way. A single account, an exact revenue of eighty-nine dollars every fiscal year for who knows how long. It is something about there being only one. My subscriber was no longer a number, not a printed address on the lower left corner of The Title's cover. A person. And he was here. Skeletal trees dot the overhead in their pitiful yard-wide plots in the concrete, surrounded with shed leaves. Cars sound their horns but I've escaped the thick of their noise. I look around the intersection, looking for my former office. Above me, a skyline extends beyond in shapes I cannot recognize. Where was I headed again? I remember the slip of paper in my pocket, but follow the sidewalk without looking down toward a line of trees.

I reach the end of a block, an intersection at which a single taxicab waits. I glance toward the lights, finding them in the driver's favor, yet the car doesn't move. When I approach, the back doors open, a man climbs out onto the curb, in the middle of unleashing a torrent of expletives at the turned head of the driver through the plexiglass. A woman, his wife, flaps her hand with anguish, lugging a swaddled infant in her other arm. I reach for my rolled sleeves, still damp with sweat, and unfurl them, not dressed for the wind. The cab speeds off. The couple and their child stand on the corner, the man gesticulating wildly. His wife begs him to calm down, putting their baby between them, still asleep. As I approach, the woman's eyes dart my way, wary.

"What kind of—leaves us out here in the cold like this? It's three goddamn miles to the hotel—"

The crosswalk flashes red, and I slow to a stop, though no cars appear at either side. For one long minute we stand, just feet apart, while they continue, in hushed tones.

"We can walk, it's not a big deal."

The man takes up loose handfuls of his hair, turning his face from me. His posture is familiar, somehow. I have seen a man do this to his head before. His wife bounces on her knees with the infant. The lights change. I stay where I am.

"Are you lost?" I ask.

"No, no," the woman answers, "we've come from the hotel."

I glance down the street, past rows of houses, their roofs obscured by the dense line of trees. The light has gone quickly.

"My husband left his wallet in our suite. When we told the cab driver, he told us to get out."

The man still hasn't looked at me. I wonder if he views the scenario as shameful, if my presence there, an able man—with a wallet—is somehow an affront to his own personhood. I glare at him, trying to make him see me.

"We'll walk," his wife says, "It's no big deal."

At that, her child wakes. We fall silent as it opens its eyes, gazes up at its mother's face, briefly, then crunches its features together and begins to howl.

"She's cold," the man says with despair, "she's going to be miserable."

His wife transfers the infant to him, removing her coat, and double-wraps the blankets with it. The infant makes no notice, continuing to scream. I glance around the houses, my breath escaping into the air as wisps of fog, and fear someone may call the police. The woman coos helplessly, making hopeful little faces met only with more screaming.

The issue, I know, contains several pages of cardstock subscription renewal inserts, including one made of a specialty plastic foil. Slightly lustrous, costing the printer triple that of our regulation cardstock, the insert had not been removed, nor could it be, given that the files had already gone to Tampa. While my ears begin to ring from the girl's noises, I produce one of the two remaining copies in my bag. The couple has forgotten me, crowded around their daughter. They stop as I open the issue, finding the insert, and tear it from the binding.

"Any chance she'd like this?" I ask, offering it up. The man scowls at me, unrestrained, but the woman takes it. She bites the thumb of her mitten off and presents the peculiar piece of paper to her daughter, "Georgia, Georgia look how shiny—"

We watch as the girl's screams subside. She blinks, curiously, at the sparkly insert, then fusses, moving her shoulders. The woman frees her arms from the blankets, and she reaches for it. Her tiny fingers close around it, crinkling the paper. When she releases it, it unfurls, without a crease. Her squeal is different, enraptured by her gift. Her parents exchange looks, their eyes come to me. I offer up the issue.

"Please, take this." I say, "The product is voided now that the insert's been removed."

The woman takes it. I watch it disappear within the folds of her purse. One left. Which was alright, I say to myself. The last I would keep safe. The girl in her arms is quiet, crushing and releasing the shiny insert over and over. A gentle snow falls overhead. The man tugs at the woman's arm, and cross the street, leaving me there. They are almost to the other side when the woman turns her head.

"Merry Christmas."

I stare after her for a moment before they are swallowed up under a faulty streetlight. "Christmas," I repeat to myself. It couldn't be Christmas. I begin to shiver.

Another mile, the snow is dry enough to blanket the sidewalk, numbing the soles of my feet. I draw my arms tightly around me, walking faster. The mailboxes tell me the house is another block at most, perhaps the next intersection. I am breathing too hard to tamp my growing elation. Despite giving up my two spare copies, my mission remains intact. I will have done something with my day. I will hand the issue personally to my last subscriber, perhaps tell him a story of The Title's last days, a magazine that once controlled a budget in the billions, its own skyscraper deep in the city. Did he know that its senior editors could once take out interest free loans directly from the publisher to purchase homes and for other large expenses? Did he know it was one of the first magazines in the world to employ women reporters? If I am lucky, I may even be invited inside, for a drink, for dinner with him and his family. What a glorious way for a friendship to start, one we could tell everybody we knew at parties.

I pass the great oak, its roots so large that they have upended the concrete slats above them, causing jagged cracks that neighbor children have chipped keepsakes from. I stand a while, looking at it, the tree over which I'd fallen off my bike at the age of seven, skinning my knee so bad that the blood had run in thick rivers down into my sock. Snow has piled around its roots. I step cautiously over. Where my bearings have before been vague, I can feel them sharpening. It occurs to me now: I've grown up here. My feet carry over the cracks and dips in the sidewalk with knowing, I walked them every day from school for the tenderest period of my childhood, before my mother left. I know these routes. I pause, overcome. I don't remember the address my supervisor had provided. I reach into my pocket for the paper and come up empty. I pat myself down, straining for a number, for letters. I search for another minute. Rather than admit I am lost, I keep walking.

I have come upon the house. And what I see at last are the trees, bare yet filling the handsome shapes I remember with their crooked branches. I raise the lever on the gate, passing through, leaving deep wells of slush in my footprints. The trees tower around me, swaying, offering little moans of age. I pull from my bag the third issue. I am climbing the porch steps. The columns are lit with the string lights from the basement. As I've grown older,

I've commandeered their arrangement, and it often occurs to me that I am now the only one who remembers to put them up anymore. I arrive at the door. I remember the key and dig it from the soil of the empty planter under the doorbell. I see myself inside, stomping my feet, leaving cakes of dirty snow in the shapes of the grooves on my boot soles.

"That you?" I hear him. His voice has come from around the corner of the stairs, the kitchen where I have commonly found some wrapped celery and peanut butter, perhaps raisins, a snack my mother left out for me after I'd already headed to school. It is strange that he'd be home.

"Yeah."

In my socks I pass the stairs, glimpsing the tree, a five-footer this year, laden with our baubles and tinsel from the green chest in the basement. I proceed into the light. My father stands with his back to the sink. A brief look around confirms there is in fact, no snack laid out for me today.

My father smiles, clasping his hands together at his waist, looking at me.

"So. No school 'til next year," he says, "How's it feel?"

I move my head to the left and right. I'm still holding the issue up to my chest. He notices it, and a shadow falls on his face. He reaches his hand out.

"Yeah . . . I'll . . . I'll take that."

I hand it to him. He sets the magazine aside, where it captures light from above within its glossy cover. I observe: that little white box. The name, my father's, the address, mistakenly switched with that of a house four hundred miles away, the place he'd really been visiting all these years for his work trips, outside it another lawn, in it another living room, another tree, a wife, children.

"How old are they?" I had asked him, when he visited my room the night my mother had gone to my aunt's. It was unknown if she'd be back to spend Christmas. My father had withdrawn his hand from my back, as I'd asked the question. He was silent. I looked at him with one eye where I lay my head on my pillow.

"The girl is four, the two boys are eight and eleven."

Perhaps this had been the moment, after it all, of my own undoing, of his. The moment I realized that his eldest son, my step-brother, was two years older than me. That I, and my mother, were the second home, and not them.

In the kitchen, my father cups the back of my neck in the dry warmth of his palm. My mother will not return. I remind her of the lie, I suppose. I have never watched her make my after-school snack; I wonder if her hands shook while she made it, if I am merely the keepsake of an evil act and that is why she does not want me anymore.

"Merry Christmas," my father says.

I nod, returning his little smile, and watch something in him crumble a little further into his foundations.

"It's late," he says, finally, "You should go to bed."

I turn around. I climb the stairs in my socks, reaching the second-floor landing and the door to my room. With my foot, I prod it open, and shake myself free of my pants and sweater, leaving them pooled on the floor. In the window is my view of the front yard between the trees, the blue fencing, the bare patch of dirt in our lawn where not even the professionals could coax new grass. I'd watched them sod the area from here, only for the next season's rains to pool there and drown it all. Sinking into my bed loosens my tight spine and I breathe the clean sheets. I observe: the corners of my bedroom converge, drawing closed, then open, like lungs. One by one the house's noises die, the hum of the radiator, the wind on walls outside, my father's footsteps on the floorboards below. I close my eyes.

THE RED HAIR

DARA YEN ELERATH

My friend Hannah liked to brush her hair. It was long, red, and slightly dry from when she'd iron it. Each day I'd watch her drag a sandalwood pick through it as though it were a horse's mane. When she'd leave my house I'd find tendrils of it everywhere: in my bed, beneath the sink, or twisted through the leaves of the old jade plant. *Hannah*, I would say, *you ought not to brush it so much*, but she was taken with a need to smooth it. At night I would dream of her hair. Once, I dreamed it was a fire she was trying to light, the sandalwood pick a match she was rubbing against a strip of phosphorus and ground glass on the side of a matchbox. Through this dream I began to understand her, to know her hair as a door she longed to open. She used so many creams and lotions, she obsessed over its texture. *If only I had hair bright and shiny as a ladybug's shell*, she would exclaim as we sat gazing through the frost-lacquered window of a January afternoon. Hannah's hair took on, for both of us, a kind of mystical significance; we spoke of it as though it were a tiger. *How is it today?* I'd ask, and she'd pet it slightly saying, *A little wild, I need to tame it.* Then she'd take out the pick and I'd comb it for her—hair like a heavy, velvet curtain or an ocean filled with red algae. Stroking it was hypnotic and we'd fall asleep. When we woke red strands would be woven through our fingers like tiny ropes. At times, it seemed the hair wanted to consume us. Some days I'd choke while eating dinner and pull from my mouth a single strand of coiled copper hair. I began to fear Hannah. At the same time the color red haunted me: stop signs, apples, roses, brick buildings, raw meat, old tubes of my mother's poppy lipstick. One time, I skinned my knee and blood that poured forth was like Hannah's hair—long strands of red I tried to gather in my hands like yarn. I rubbed the strands against my cheeks for luck, but when my mother saw me she only screamed, she said I was sick and scrubbed my face with scalding water. *Daughter, daughter, moon and psalter*, I used to chant each month when my period began; this was to summon Hannah. But my mother claimed I never had such a friend. She held my hand over the stove to try and rouse me. *Wake up*, she shouted, shaking me. When she did this I saw streaks of red behind my eyes. Copper coiling into gold coiling into copper.

CELEBRATION

BENJAMIN BARTU

it filters through like some unwarranted glare, accident
involving ring-necked pheasant passed on the road to the sea,
like the unfortunately named flower fields from which on
clear mornings canola oil can be seen to drip, a sign spotted
in the midst of wilderness

   children's reading centre this way

pointing into suspiciously barren tracts of land, the character
of this emptiness reminding you of last night's chickening alone
in your bed, where half your flightless nonsense set to twitching,
your head cocked back, your concentration devoting itself anew
to the challenge of staying conscious, of remaining awake in your plot
of dark, which collapses again the question of have you learned to live
with yourself, and share your brain with the parts you didn't choose,
which have outlived you already despite best intentions, idea of ugliness,
needfulness, so many seizures, so many villages, you have come now
to Sheringham, one more seaside where you still have not found a taste
for peppermint tea, but it's what Peter has offered so you drink, his house
disintegrating around you, green-brown twiggy things fluttering toward
your lips, your mind-body opposition flaring for the second time in twelve
hours when Ko Ko says

   do you know there is a dove in your living room

to which of course Peter says he knew no such thing despite
having been here since waking, strolling around the apartment
with a family pack of fun size chocolate bars under one arm, and
he sets them down now to look behind the sofa and sure enough
there it is, winking at the window, one eye permanently shut to the peace
process of the world

[the other refusing to leave the clouds]

and Su, who is looking at a book called *The Anxiety of Photography*
takes out her phone and immediately begins snapping pictures of the bird
while you watch and think on how the two of you don't talk much,
really, but maybe you know one another in some small way since a year
ago she woke in her own dark to find all hearing in her right ear gone,
afflicted by a condition known as sudden sensorineural hearing loss, SSHL
for short, although this sense of camaraderie is threadbare and based
only in the knowledge that both of your bodies have betrayed you

[a camaraderie you share with the dove, struck still in fear]

you watch the bird for minutes, then it weaves its second magic, the trick
of beautiful things, survival mechanism of suddenly becoming utterly
dull, beauty incapable of remaining its own excuse for being for long, and so
you walk through town to the cliffside overlooking the shore scattered
with pebbles

they use the seastone here to adorn the buildings

they have a certain ageless banality, and are coveted, so much so that nearby
cities have requested shipments of the pebbles, but as you get farther
inland, much as anything is inland anymore, the cost of transportation
spikes, and so there are fewer rocks to go around, and so holier and holier
become the buildings worthy of their decoration, sacred as city halls, sacred
pebble castles ornamenting London, nowadays, after a high tide the beach
is covered in plastics

the seals don't come in so much

so you bend and grip a stone, inspect it in your palm, or pretend to, until
the first magic comes again and you find yourself, what could be your true
self, loving its utter mediocrity, its indistinctness among pebble-kind,
the smoothness of its orbit

[and that's the disco, isn't it]

burning you with its reason, slipping off you like a sheet, finding you
in the night like the figure of a pedestrian ahead who stops at the sound
of your step, turns, and bids you pass like an answer into empty yet,
like you're someone who gives a damn when they get home, not yet walked
out of wishes, deserving alive

SECOND PERSON

CHRISTINE BOYER

There are things you know.

    You know, for example, that when a family member calls you right before noon on a regular Friday in October, the news isn't going to be good. No one calls you on a weekday afternoon aside from automated appointment reminders, so you know the family member on the other line is going to say "I'm so sorry" at least three times. You know your response to them ("wait, *what?*"), repeated over and over, is just your brain buying you time to catch up to what they are saying.

    You know you need to pack quickly, so you throw every piece of black clothing you own into your suitcase. Your mother's voice, always echoing in your head, disapproves: that dress is too short, that shirt shows too much cleavage. How can you be a thirty-two-year old woman with a mortgage and a master's degree and still not own any sensible closed-toe shoes? You load your suitcase and your bewildered dog into your car, then speed the entire way across Ohio, across the thin arm of West Virginia that rests companionably along Pennsylvania. You arrive home.

    You know you have a role to play. Supportive older sister. Eldest child. The no-nonsense one. In the days to come, people will tell you that they aren't worried about you because you are strong. They do not see—how could they?—everything that lies ahead for you. The panic attacks in traffic after driving past a fender bender. The desperate see-sawing between insomnia and twelve-hour long naps. The sudden craving for Cap'n Crunch at two in the morning that leaves you bawling, because the grocery stores are closed and you aren't really crying about cereal anyway.

You arrive home. The house is full of people, arranged in hushed clusters around the dining room and kitchen, and all you want to do is usher them out, slide the deadbolt behind them. They come and hug you: the aunts and uncles and second cousins and neighbors, these grief tourists and rubber-neckers. You let them pull you close and whisper the usual, tired sentiments about being in a better place and God calling home an angel. You take note of the dandruff on the shoulders of their cheap acrylic sweaters, the lipstick on their teeth. You turn your head from their stale breath reeking of gas station coffee and Parliaments.

One by one, the neighbors and coworkers leave, and only family remains. You watch them huddle around the kitchen table, their voices low. A phrase floats up in your brain, *keeping the deathwatch*, and you wonder where it came from. They talk about themselves—this one's thyroid cancer, that one's shot transmission in their Ford. They slowly circle to the topic everyone has been avoiding.

"I saw the car," says your aunt. She lives in the same town where the crash happened, and she had been sitting at a stop light when the wrecker came through. "I thought it looked just like Brenda's car."

And so, they are given the facts as you know them: at approximately 6:58 in the morning, on Friday, October 25, your mother was traveling north on Route 36 in Eldred Township, Jefferson County. She was traveling in her blue Hyundai Sonata when a nineteen-year-old coming the other way lost control of his silver Hyundai Elantra, crossed the center line, and hit her. Or rather, she hit him, head-on to his passenger side. He survived the crash; she did not. She was fifty-six years old, having celebrated her last birthday only eleven days prior.

These are the things you know.

When I was a freshman in college, I had an English professor who railed against second person narration. Nothing set her off more than the "you" point of view, and woe to the student who experimented with it.

Second person, she said, was cheap. Lazy. It was a shortcut to making the reader feel something when the writer wasn't skilled enough to evoke feelings any other way.

Sure, it can be cheap and lazy. It can be tedious, especially when it carries through an entire piece or, heaven forbid, an entire novel.

But the second person can also be a sort of armor in memoir pieces—a way to put distance between the writer and the subject who are, after all, the same person. It can be a coping mechanism. It's easier to say "you" went through this terrible thing instead of "me." You are the daughter of a difficult mother who died suddenly, not me. Not me—you.

The second person is not a way to make you feel here. It's a way to stop me from feeling. If it's you and not me, then I can keep bumping along with my own life, mundane and unremarkable. A life filled with weeknight dinners in a slow cooker, walks with my rescue dogs, weekends lost to *Law and Order: SVU* marathons on cable. I don't need to obsess anymore with my mother about the minutiae of my life—or the larger questions—now that she isn't in it.

You feel these things. Not me.

There are things you learn, over time.

You learn, for example, that your mother was listening to Bob Seger at the time of her death. She had received a CD of his greatest hits for her birthday, and she had taken it with her that morning to listen to on her drive.

You learn about Bob Seger when you go to the junkyard where the ruined cars are waiting for release from the state police investigation. When you walk up to the crushed Sonata, you smell gasoline and something else—something floral. It takes you a moment to recognize her perfume (Wind Song) and you have to steady yourself against the car from the gut-punch it delivers.

On the floor of your mother's car, among the broken glass and shards of plastic and one bloody latex glove, is the shattered CD case.

You can guess which song she was listening to. How many hours of your childhood did you listen to the same song, over and over and over, because she never let a cassette play through? How many times did she rewind "Born in the USA" to play "Cover Me" a million times in a row? How many times did you hear "Crocodile Rock" or "Message in a Bottle" or the live-from-Hawaii version of "Can't Help Falling in Love"?

You'd bet your life that she was listening to "Night Moves" when she was crushed to death on a Friday morning.

There are things you'll never know. They are things that sit with you like the hard sliver of a popcorn kernel that slides between the gum and the molar.

You tongue at them, at the swollen gum line, trying to pry them free. You are a person that likes knowing things for the sake of knowing them. Questions without answers rankle you. Those little pieces of popcorn kernels, for example? Those are called the pericarp. You looked it up because not knowing it irritated you.

You'll never know where the cold rage springs from inside you. It bounded out of you, a wellspring of anger, when the parents of the nineteen-year-old responsible for the crash came to your mother's viewing. The funeral home was emptied out, and the funeral director ushered them in: the father in a tan Carhartt jacket, the mother in a sweatshirt emblazoned with the local high school's mascot. You hate that one of your high school teachers, a latecomer to the viewing, was there to witness the whole sorry scene, muttering "oh my, oh my" over and over. You hate that your sister walked the nineteen-year-old's mother over to your mother, laid out in her casket. You hate that the woman called your mother beautiful. You wanted to yank back the crocheted afghan that covers your mother from the chest down, you wanted to make the woman bear witness. *Massive trauma to the chest and lower extremities*, as the police report said. Not so beautiful now, right?

You'll never know why your relationship with your mother was so complicated. You'll go to grief counseling, art therapy, talk therapy. You'll spend so much time in talk therapy, so much money. The amount of money you'll spend will shame you, especially since you came from a family that views medical doctors with suspicion, let alone mental health professionals.

You'll learn about inherited trauma. Together, you and your therapist will chart out a genetic legacy of pain and mental illness: a motherless great-grand-mother, punted across the Atlantic between her father in America and her aunts in Italy. A grandmother given up for adoption, who ran from the county official when she saw him waiting for her on her front porch. A grandfather who went to Korea as a baby-faced boy and came back with PTSD before the term even existed. A mother with clinical depression, an eating disorder, maybe narcissistic personality disorder. A straight line across a hundred years, pointing straight to you: a girl who eats her feelings who turned into a woman so anxious that the muscles in her neck are on perma-lock.

"If I have kids, will they have issues too?" you'll ask your therapist. She will give you that enigmatic half-smile they must teach psychologists in college. She doesn't answer.

It is another thing you'll never know. You'll never have children, and that decision sits so lightly on your mind that you never reconsider it once your mind is made up.

Grief has split me into two people: the first me, and the second me. The first me kept her mother at arm's length to avoid being hurt. The first me always assumed there'd be time to fix things. There would be a death bed reconciliation, I had figured, just like in books and movies.

The second me knows that even if that nineteen-year-old hadn't lost control of his car, things wouldn't have changed. There would always be the push/pull relationship of a depressed mother and an anxious daughter, too much alike in some ways and too different in others. What I needed from her was mothering, to be comforted and assured it would all be okay. It was the one thing she couldn't give me. How can you give comfort when you yourself need to be comforted? How can you be a mother when you need to be mothered yourself? There was too much accumulated trauma in our DNA, too much suffering to untangle in a single lifetime.

There will be a moment, years after your mother's death. You'll be at the emergency room, nursing a migraine so painful that you will sign off on anything—a spinal tap, a medically-induced coma, a hole drilled in the skull—for relief. You'll spend the first two hours in the waiting room, swathed in giant sunglasses to avoid the glare of the TV blaring *Cops*. You'll spend the next two hours trying to convince the triage nurse that you are not looking to score opiates.

When you finally get a bed, when the nurse finally finds a vein and starts the liquid ibuprofen and sedative, there will be a moment. You'll close your eyes, alone, and you'll feel it—a hand on your forehead, for the briefest second. A flood of scent, florals with a bit of amber and musk, the perfume from your childhood. And a thought, unbidden, that rises to the top of the mind above the throbbing pain of the migraine: It's all okay.

You'll feel these things. Not me.

A Response to a Pair of Forest Plots

Derek Sheffield

is my assignment. But all the firs
in the first that was clear-cut and
replanted huddle thick together
exactly alike, exactly where twenty
years ago each was boot-stamped
to grow into this big dark box.

And while the second was thinned
then—less crowded with intent, a little light
spilling through—I can't help
but see every sizable tree still grows
right where someone
shook a rattle can and sprayed.

Something else entirely
here in the roadside ditch
                   in blue ruffled dabs
         among the untidy
     grasses—wild
irises, where I kneel
       to better see
         white starbursts veined
with lines thin as moth legs
         upon the splayed sepals—
and feel   the slight space
     held by the petals
         that curl up and in like
tongues toward one other,
        touch
   without touching,
      and hold.

THE GIRL WHO CRIED FLOWERS

R. R. PINTO

The story was called "The Girl Who Cried Flowers." We read it aloud as a class, each taking turns under the beady eyes of Sister Mary Helene. But I'd read it already, many times, to myself. In the story, a girl cried flowers instead of tears. At first it was lovely, but later, the condition became an annoyance to those around her. She fell in love with a young man who said it didn't matter to him. But in the end, she realized that it really did. The last scene was of her, running away and crying, real tears streaming from her eyes at last.

The idea of flowers falling from a beautiful woman's eyes enchanted me. While the class droned on, I started to draw the flowers on the pages of my workbook—fanciful, many-whorled blossoms, as beautiful as I could make them. Some had even-pointed heads with round centers, while others formed the soft swirls of a rose. Then there were those that didn't belong to any genus—the flowers of my dreams. Exquisite and intricate, like a fairy tale—all of the beauty I could muster with my #2 pencil.

Through my visions, I saw the girl at the next desk raise her hand.

"Sister!" Patty Gill pointed at me. "She isn't paying attention. She's drawing birds and flowers on her book. I saw her!"

My body clenched as the whole third grade class turned to look at me. I'd like to think I spoke up, explaining that I was listening to the story and illustrating it. I'd like to imagine that Sister Mary Helene told Patty Gill to mind her own business.

But here's what really happened: After a moment of blank panic, I started to erase my ugly flowers with wide frantic strokes, my head bent in shame. I couldn't meet Patty's eyes, smug across the aisle. I couldn't meet Sister's eyes, their solemnity sprinkled with distaste, like salt on a hard-boiled egg. I certainly couldn't meet my classmates' eyes, their communal force making my head fuzzy. I felt like I had radiation.

As I erased holes into my paper, I silently willed everyone to look away. Sister Mary Helene averted her eyes and said, "Children, you should always pay attention in class. Patty, I think it's your turn to read next." She'd skipped over my turn, and I spent the rest of the class listening quietly. I never drew flowers in my workbook again.

That moment of exposure meant that I hadn't done things right. As a result, I was noticed. I'd given people the opportunity to see me, to see our differences. In the years that followed, I made sure that rarely happened again.

Erasing yourself just enough to achieve a bland reaction is an art form. It's a slippery endeavor that takes years of honing and demands absolute dedication. I knew I'd succeeded when I was a sophomore in high school. A girl who lived nearby complained to me about all of the Indian people who were moving into our neighborhood. "White people like us are getting crowded out by all those immigrants," she said to me. Immigrant—a word to hide from, a word that revealed what I really was. I moved to the U.S. from the Philippines when I was three. I arrived scared and mute, unable to recognize the words or people around me. But I learned.

Throughout college and adulthood, I polished my skill with increasing expertise. I watched and I copied. I chose just the right clothes. I joined a sorority. I dated white boys with white-sounding names. I turned away from Filipino food and served ham biscuits at my wedding. I erased everything I could that made me an "other."

This achieved the goal I'd set so many years ago, before my brain was even fully formed. All I knew then was that I didn't want to feel different anymore. I didn't want to be an outsider. I didn't want to be an immigrant. I wanted to be safe. I wanted to belong.

I didn't realize then that there was a price to pay, that I'd become so good at self-effacement, that I wouldn't know how to ask for things or how to stand up and say, "See me. Hear me."

It's been several weeks since the world watched a black man call for his mother while someone else kneeled on his neck, squeezing the air and the life out of his body. There was public outrage. There was sadness, despair, and

THE GIRL WHO CRIED FLOWERS

fear. And I think for many of us, there was shame. I have had to ask myself a question: How much am I willing to risk?

How much am I willing to stand up as a brown woman and yell, loudly and clearly, "Black Lives Matter!" How much am I willing to call attention to the very thing I've tried to neutralize my entire life? How much am I willing to say, "See me. Hear me"? And what if I don't do it right? What if I say the wrong thing? What if the attention I receive is negative and judgmental? Is the cost worth it?

But deep inside, I know. What we risk is inconsequential compared to what black people risk just by being. Staying frozen while trying to compose just the right words and just the right actions is a luxury not everyone has. The brave thing, the right thing, is to speak up, to be seen, to go in and know that you will probably mess up, but that the alternative—silence—provides no chance for improvement.

It's time to draw my flowers on the page.

I don't know what they will look like, after so many years of erasure. Perhaps, as in the story, they will turn into tears.

LE *RÊVE*, HENRI ROUSSEAU
ANDREA JURJEVIĆ

The window, propped open by bottles of Grolsch, frames the night sky.

Leaves of Zanzibar gem, thick and erect, reach for the sky like human hands,
  while you, dressed in moonlight, place *Lush Life* on the record player. I
  like how the green

absorbs me—the large print on the wall, its hothouse jungle twitch, the
  snake in the undergrowth, the flute player, creatures with raised muzzles
  rubbing palm fronds, the woman on the sofa, her skin of wild honey, as
  naked as me on the bed below her,

also someone's misplaced animal. And what does she teach me?

There's never a bad time to wear lipstick.

We all author and haunt our own dreams.

This may or may not be us. This gash of the feral, the painter's last green
  reverie.

Pillow Talk with Modigliani's *Kneeling Blue Caryatid*

Andrea Jurjević

In his mind's eye there was no room for background, her dress on the floor,
    or a dumb fruit bowl her hand dipped into, nothing

but Akhmatova's cosmic geometry. He took in each curve and shadow of her
    body to the point that within her light he saw an entire world—свет
    within свéтлый.

It's as if he kissed the glistening mouth of those galaxies and knocked them
    back until they were all he knew. Drunk, euphoric artist. Just like god

must be asleep in his recliner, dreaming of us coiling like a twist of citrus in
    his midnight drink.

mermaid

JOEL FISHBANE

Iris meets Capp_Gibb online and for two weeks he doesn't tell her he's in Afghanistan and she doesn't tell him she can't speak. It's Gibb who cracks first. There will be a new rotation at the end of November and he's coming home. Would she like to meet? His sign-off is like an extra piece of exposition, added in case she missed the point: *Gibb Callaghan, 1rst Infantry, Camp Nathan Smith.*

Iris fields the message while dying in a fundraising meeting. She plays the clarinet and, looking for extra credit, she's agreed to be in the band for *The Little Mermaid.* The university has cut their funding and now the group needs to figure out how to pay for rollerblades and fins. Iris isn't listening to the talk of bake sales and lotteries. She's reading, or rather re-reading, Gibb's confession. He told her he was overseas for work. He claimed to be in *sales.* Men and their stories. Best to play the ghost and move on. Iris is waist-deep in a double major in math and music. Midterms are on the horizon, the play opens in a month, and an essay on George Gershwin is due next week. No. She doesn't have time for Gibb Callaghan from Camp Nathan Smith.

"Iris, what do you think? Are you in?"

Iris glances up at Professor Wells, who runs the drama group and enjoys peering at everyone over the rim of his glasses. Everyone else is peering at her too. She nods and smiles.

"Great!" says Wells. "We need all the talent we can get."

No one there knows ASL and it takes a few minutes to deduce her mistake. Last year's talent show was a hit, and no one has the creativity to think of something new. Iris scrambles to undo the damage, but it's no good. She's at the school on a partial scholarship and has won awards. Claiming she doesn't like to perform is like the little mermaid saying she doesn't like to swim. But it isn't performing Iris dislikes. It's performing *alone*. Even her solos were all performed in the safety of an orchestra. Iris supposes she could refuse but the extra credit will let her graduate early and Wells has the power of the grade: he could ruin her GPA with a stroke of the pen. Goodbye scholarship. "You can do some cute Disney medley!" he says and Iris bristles. Iris doesn't do cute and she definitely doesn't play Disney by choice. Annoyed with Wells, she glances back at her phone where Gibb's confession awaits a reply. She blocks him; this is his fault too.

On her way home, Iris stops at Jean-Talon Market, which is only minutes from where she lives. The harvest of farmers has taken over. Plaid-shirts and overalls fill the aisles, hocking their abundance. The farmers haven't yet moved indoors, despite the recent rain, and Iris is able to wander in the pale November light, stopping to sample cut-up cheddar and homemade *confiture*. She's at home among the harvest, an echo of a youth spent cycling past farmers and road-side stalls. She's been in Montreal for almost three years but it's impossible to feel homesick with the market in her backyard. Iris takes a selfie with a prized squash that weighs seventy pounds and posts it at once (#miraclesquash #jeantalon #montreal). She's new to Instagram but she's already a fan; she likes the speed of the thing and it's been a great way to get more eyes on her blog.

A text arrives from her sister. *That's some squash.*

Iris makes a happy face with punctuation. Then: *Gibb is army. Afghanistan. Men in uniform. Beware.*

I know, right? What are you up to?

Looking up train fares, writes Justine. *I think I'm going home.*

Uh-oh, thinks Iris. She drafts a few responses but, in the end, doesn't reply.

Their mother always said that getting a good deal is the whole point of a farmer's market and when Iris leaves, she knows she's done the ghost proud. At home, she posts a picture of her haul (#harvest #jeantalon #montreal) before putting the food away. The apartment is a tomb. Anne-Marie's boyfriend likes her enough to let her stay there but not enough to put her name on the lease. She's rarely home, which makes it easy for Iris to pretend she's single in the city. She hasn't done much with this freedom except haunt dating apps and leave the kitchen a mess. Now she digs out her sheet music and starts gathering the Gershwin tunes. He's been her idol ever since she first heard that clarinet warble which opens *Rhapsody in Blue*. Cracking into an apple, she sorts through the possibilities. He wrote musicals and concertos. He was all about the jazz. Her essay is biographical, and Iris already knows the research by heart. Born in 1898. Middle child. No one thought he'd amount to anything. Such a wonderful beginning.

Iris puts aside the music and googles pictures of Camp Nathan Smith. Named for a private who was killed eight years ago in an incident of friendly fire. So many ways to die. Some future soldier might write to some future girl about life in Camp Gibson Callaghan. Who she ghosted and became a ghost himself. Notifications interrupt her browsing. The world approves of her prized squash. A man on Heartmates offers a wave and a message. *Nice face. Hate the hair. Has it changed?* Iris writes back that it has. *In fact, I'm shaving my head as we speak.* She blocks the user and scrolls on. Gibb's last message festers, a communication now DOA and ready to be put out of its misery. His last girlfriend, he wrote, broke up with him because she couldn't deal with the uncertainty. Conversely, there are women for whom his job is his only appeal. Army-fuckers. People who believe they have a patriotic duty to support the troops any way they can. Is it any wonder he kept the truth to himself? This isn't an excuse, he added. Just context.

A medley, she decides, isn't a bad idea. She can combine her favorites. *A Foggy Day. Swanee.* Love songs, to be sure, but not the saccharine kind. Sucking on a reed—she's breaking it in—Iris arranges the music and begins making cuts, already imagining how she'll segue from one song to the next. As a boy, Gershwin roller-skated through traffic. His parents bought the piano for his brother, but he made it his own. At a music store, he plugs other people's songs, all the while thinking, I can do that. And three years later he publishes his first song. From the beginning, he stormed through life, claiming it as his own. Iris is twenty. When Gershwin was twenty, Al Jolson was singing *Swanee* on Broadway. What has Iris done? Panicked over her GPA and posed with a giant squash. Still, by all accounts, Gershwin was a scamp. Lots of girlfriends. An illegitimate son, depending on what you believe. All men are uncertain. In or out of uniform.

She skypes Justine, positioning the webcam so it can capture her hands. *I think I should write him*, she signs.

"Are you looking to be talked into it or out of it? Because if he's going to be important, we'll need to give him a sign."

Iris makes the sign for a soldier, pretending to hold a rifle that she thumps against her chest. Usually, the right hand forms an A but Iris makes a G. Justine repeats it, nodding in approval. Like any good nickname, it needs to flow off the hands.

I accidentally agreed to be in a talent show. Performing by myself.

"Alone? When's the heart attack?"

Any moment now. Then Iris adds, *Don't go home.*

"It's fine. I'll wait until Dad's out of town."

The sign for "Dad" involves touching the thumb to the forehead as if creating a fin, so the rest of the hand is extended outward. Justine and Iris have long adapted this gesture—they touch their foreheads with a fist that has the middle finger raised. This flows off the hands too.

So, it's not a visit, it's a robbery.

"He's either going to sell Mom's things or throw them away."

And if you see Mrs. B?

"Who knows? Maybe I'll try to save her from herself. Not that it'll work. Every time I talk, I just come off as the angry daughter of Ellington Cook."

Still waiting for advice about Gibb.

Beware men in uniform, signs Justine.

Later, Iris tests the new reed and takes the proposed medley for a spin. She doesn't need the music, but she watches it anyway, making mental notes of where she can slip free. The paradox of Iris is that she likes the safety of the orchestra but not its constraints; she wants musicians to surround her but not if they're going to tell her what to do. It's her great challenge, one which every teacher has seen. "Your problem is you like to chatter," Mrs. B had once said. Chatter? Iris thought this was a mistake. But Mrs. B was not the kind to misspeak. "Some musicians want to be told what to say," she said. "You want to talk, talk, talk."

Now, all these years later, Iris wants to tell Mrs. B how right she was. She supposes there will be plenty of chances. The wedding's in the spring. Mrs. B will be her stepmother now, not quite the wicked one of stories, but a stepmother all the same. Assuming Justine doesn't put a stop to things. Justine thinks Mrs. B would make a different choice if given the chance. She's misinformed. Like those people who only watch one news channel. Like me and

Gibb, Iris thinks. We've both been living off lies, giving our daydreams the wrong setting and cast. Iris puts down the music and goes back to her phone. She unblocks Gibb and writes her reply; she sends it before she can change her mind.

The auction is at Gert's, the student pub, and on the night of the talent show, Iris trudges to the bar and envisions the torture ahead. She slept poorly last night and today anxiety is weighing her down. The pub has a comforting shabby air, with old chairs and echoes of renovations done years before. A set of risers form the makeshift stage and Iris joins the other talents who Professor Wells has corralled into the event. The pianist writes poetry. The redhead playing Ariel, the eponymous mermaid, claims to be a stand-up comic. Iris ducks into the bathroom and throws up. Water only but it leaves a sour taste that she worries will stain her reed. Great. She'll be tasting her fear for days. In the mirror, she rinses her mouth and stares at her reflection. Nothing but color and frump, she thinks. It's been two weeks since she contacted Gibb; he still hasn't replied. The almost-ghost has become the definitely-ghosted.

Backstage, Iris paces while the show proceeds. She clutches her phone for security—something about its solidity keeps her tethered to the ground. She's already blocked Gibb again. Punishment for his silence. Suddenly, she's struck by a tragic thought. He's a man at war. Suppose she was ghosted because he *really* was a ghost? Would she ever know? She'll have to check the news for casualty reports. Or maybe she's reaching. Ockham's razor. The likeliest answer is usually the truth. She told Gibb about her condition. In her experience, her silence usually begets more. Yet she can't help but wonder. Suppose she disappoints simply because she's disappointing? Nice face. Hate the hair.

Her phone vibrates. Iris frowns. It's her father, poking his head out, like the groundhog searching for sun. She has a sudden intuition that this has to do with the wedding and Mrs. B and Justine. On stage, Professor Wells plays emcee. He's the bubbly born-for-the-spotlight type and cracks knowing jokes. "Our next act comes to us straight from the woodwind section of our little orchestra. Like Ariel, she sold her voice to a sea witch but, fortunately, they let her keep her clarinet." Iris tucks the phone away; there's no time to deal with it now.

Applause. Iris waves. The clarinet shakes in her hand. There's no chair and no sheet music. Nothing between her and the world. She dons the one prop she brought for the occasion: a woman's fedora, whose brim she pulls low over eyes. Partly to block out the world. Partly because, well, it's just plain cool. She shuts her eyes and begins. The opening of *Rhapsody in Blue*. A trill followed by seventeen diatonic notes in rapid succession. Like a heartbeat springing to life. She shifts into *A Foggy Day*. Gershwin had nerves. He called it his composer's stomach. Yet he performed all the time. At the San Francisco Symphony Orchestra, he forgot the notes for *Concerto in F* because of the brain tumor in his head. Still, he carried on. Iris carries on too. When she's done, the applause lifts the weight she's been carrying all day; it even sounds sincere.

Iris dares to lift the fedora's brim so she can look into the crowd. At a table near the front, sitting by himself, one young man applauds louder than the rest. They lock eyes and he offers a devil's grin. He's fit and strong with a head like a shorn lamb. An army cut. He looks like his picture. The one she still looks at even though she blocked him days before.

Her work done, she escapes backstage where she tries to disassemble the clarinet with shaking hands. Perhaps, she thinks, it isn't really him. Men in the army get the same haircut; it could be some jarhead home from abroad. Her act is followed by two actors rehashing the old Abbot and Costello sketch about who's on first, and only when it's done is she able to slip back into the crowd. No. It's him. Gibb motions to the empty chair at his table. Iris stares. This can't be some wild coincidence. Behind her, Professor Wells introduces the poetic pianist. Iris takes the seat but shifts the chair so there's more space between her and Capp_Gibb.

"My laptop got shot up by the Taliban," he whispers. "You'd blocked me by the time I got back online."

Well, it's better than saying the dog ate his homework. Iris puts her finger to her mouth and pretends to be interested in the pianist's poetry, even though he has the audacity to rhyme "death" with "flesh." There's one more act after that—a tap dance number involving the stagehands—and then Professor Wells is saying goodnight and reminding everyone to keep buying drinks because the production gets half the sales at the bar. The lights come up and the room becomes loud with conversation. Gibb leans in and asks if he can support the arts and buy her a drink.

Taking out her phone, Iris opens her notebook app. *Explain*, she types.

"Facebook," he shrugs. "Your profile said you were attending this thing. The event page did the rest." She can tell he's proud of himself; he's boasting like Sherlock Holmes at the end of the mystery, telling Watson how it was all done. "Go on," he says. "Tell me I'm a romantic."

It's a little stalker-ish, writes Iris.

"*You* blocked *me*," Gibb says. "And I wanted to apologize."

E-mail!!! Iris wishes she could underline the word, including the punctuation.

"It was a *gesture*," he says. "Like in the movies. I wanted to hear you play."

He folds in on himself and pouts. Can something be both romantic *and* stalker-ish? Iris taps her nails against her phone. *How was I?*

"Good. Great. I mean, I don't know music, but it sounded like you hit all the right notes."

Hardly high praise. But at least it's sincere. Again, he asks her if he should support the arts or if she wants him to leave. Iris considers, turning the fedora over in her hands. *Was your laptop really shot up?*

Gibb looks away. "Nah. I just got stupid. It threw me, you know? I shouldn't have thought about it. I liked writing to you. And you didn't think about it when I told you where I really was. You accepted it right away."

Iris twists her mouth. She points to the bar and raises an index finger. *One drink.*

Over a pair of Molsons, he tells her how he was raised in the West Island in an enclave of Anglophones. Divorce and time divided his family and these days his sister is the only one left. He shows her pictures. Diedre is sturdy and narrow. She works in pathology and spends all day bringing out the dead. It worries him. She's become a hard person, a woman built of brick. Gibb has seen people become detached and thinks he can spot the same vacancy behind Diedre's gaze that he sees in men with PTSD. Does *he* have PTSD? Iris wonders. She watches his eyes, trying to spot that vacancy he describes.

She's still talking with her phone and Gibb notices when her father texts again. The name and message light up the screen. *Where are you? Text me now!* Another message follows on its heels and then one more. Iris snatches the phone and puts it away. She fishes out her notebook and pen.

"You should talk to him if it's important," says Gibb.

We don't really get along, Iris scrawls.

"Only get one father."

Long story.

Gibb's curiosity melts into a shrug. "Save it. First date conversations are supposed to be fun and games."

Is this a date?

Gibb turns red. "I guess not." He drains his beer and stands to get his coat. She takes his arm before he can leave and widens her grin. "Wait. You were joking?"

Iris makes her hand flat and wiggles it back and forth.

"Sort of?" he says and Iris nods. "Sort of a date? Yeah, I guess that's about right."

He sits back down. Iris clutches her drink. He peels his label and they glance around the room. Oh, God. She should have let him leave. Now they've run out of things to say.

"Did you really sell your voice to a witch?" he asks.

Iris shrugs and nods. It's as good a story as any and she'd rather stick with the fun and games.

Gibb rolls the torn label between his fingers. "Is the musical like the movie? Do you love working on it?"

Actually, the musical is a lot like the movie and she hates both. She even has a blog post to prove it. She doesn't think Professor Wells has seen it and has a vague fear he might penalize her for apostasy. Iris gestures for his phone and finds her blog online. She watches him as he reads. In the movie, Ariel is so bewildered about living without her voice. "You'll have your looks!" cackles the sea witch. "And don't underestimate the importance of body language!" And what about literacy? Ariel can sign her name; surely, she can figure out how to write Prince Eric a note. In *Titus Andronicus*, Lavinia's rapists cut off her hands and rip out her tongue so she can't identify them. She finds a *stick* and writes their names in the *dirt*. There's also a whole song in which a cartoon crab tries to get Eric to kiss the girl. Why can't the girl kiss him instead? A voice, wrote Iris, is not a brain. Both the movie and musical tell little girls they don't need to speak to win a prince. They just need their bodies. But body language is only important if you use it say something of worth.

A lot of people argue with her interpretation. "It's a kid's story!" is the common refrain. But Gibb is intrigued. There are other Disney princesses; he wants her to dissect them all. Her phone buzzes again. More messages from her father. Gibb watches her slip into airplane mode.

"Do you get along with your mother?" he asks.

She died, writes Iris in her notebook. *He's getting remarried.*

"And you don't approve?"

Iris's pen hovers over the page. *Dad isn't always so nice.*

"I get you." Gibb checks his watch. "Are you all right getting home? Should we call you a cab?"

I usually walk. Iris twists the fedora in her hand. So. The night is over. She watches him as he collects his coat. He sounds like his emails, which counts for something. It's promising, assuming any of it can be believed. But would he really go through so much trouble o perpetuate a lie? There are other girls he could be chasing if he was interested in other things. Iris swallows the rest of the drink. You can beware men in uniform or you can roller-skate through traffic. Even Ariel, trope that she is, didn't stay under the sea.

Do you want to walk with me? she writes.

Gibb is enthusiastic even after she warns him that it's a long way to Little Italy. She adds that it's hard for her to walk and talk since it really means walking and writing. She's bound to make mistakes. But Gibb doesn't mind.

"It's a sort-of date," he says. "Let's agree to ignore our mistakes."

They set off together into the bite of November, wrapped in their fall coats and colored scarves. It's too complicated for her to tear into Disney so they talk of other things. Iris is slow and Gibb is patient and she teaches him a few simple signs, but because it's dark, he comes up with a simple aural code: one snap means yes, two means no. Even so, the conversation is stilted. Thoughts broken, quips delayed. They take a selfie outside Schwartz's Deli and stop to rest in Parc des Ameriques where, Gibb tells her, the beer tent for the Fringe Festival is set up every June. This is news to Iris, who always goes back to Justine right after exams.

"You need to think about staying. There's nothing like Montreal in the summer. A whole different kind of heat than you get in Afghanistan. And a lot more fun things to look at. I'll bet you look great in the summer. *Greater,*" he adds quickly. "You already look great."

Iris finds a fresh page. *If I'm here next summer, you show me around.*

"Actually, I might be going back."

"Oh," says Iris, though she actually mouths the word—it's a movement of the lips, followed by a light brush of air.

"Word is Canada's going to withdraw combat troops next year. Probably go into training mode to help the Afghan army. I'm a dual citizen—Dad's from Rochester—so I could re-enlist. Diedre thinks I should. But I don't know. I didn't really think about things when I joined. I needed money and I saw a poster. I like the work. But it's tough over there. I guess if there's going to be a war, they might as well have good people fighting it and if I'm a good soldier than maybe I have an obligation to keep doing it. And I gotta admit: it's a hell of an adventure."

He delivers a boyish grin. She can picture him playing warrior. The imp with the gun.

"I don't like that I'm not supposed to ask a lot of questions. It's like when I used to go to church. I wasn't supposed to ask questions then either. They always wanted me to be you."

Iris points to herself, eyebrows arched.

"You know..." He draws an imagined zipper over his mouth. "Truth is, I already read your post about the Little Mermaid. I read your whole blog. I started following you online once you told me your real name. I shouldn't have said that. Is that also stalker-ish? I sort-of looked you up and then I was down the rabbit hole. All night I've been watching your face. You never shut up. In the army, shutting up is all I do. A voice is not a brain, but I don't feel like I've been using either."

Iris looks out into the city, quiet now as midnight descends. For once, her silence is natural—she's embarrassed by this lack of a ready response. She has to fight to keep from taking his hand. If Gibb is an illusion, if he's all uniform without substance, then he's definitely mastered the trick.

Too tired for a serious convo, she writes.

"Sure," says Gibb. "Back to fun and games."

He's disappointed. He'd wanted real advice. She bites her lip as they continue up Saint-Laurent, trundling past Mont-Royal as they're heading north. Her hands are chilled from writing and she has to bundle herself into her pockets, breaking up their conversation even more. Gibb tries to take it with good humor and Iris wonders if she's being enjoyed or endured. As they reach her street, she again feels anxiety's weight. Anne-Marie is likely with her boyfriend. Given the long walk, it will seem rude not to invite Gibb in.

She tries to catch sight of her reflection in car windows. Her hair has been flattened by her hat; she's red-eyed and snotty from the cold. Yes, they've just met, but in a way they haven't. They've been talking for weeks. Even so. Perhaps she's a curiosity. The mermaid plucked from the water, the novelty to entertain him while he figures himself out.

Iris lives on the top floor of a duplex and points out her building and that's when they see someone is waiting on the stoop. A hulking shape waits on the spiraled stairs that leads to the second floor. The shape rises as they approach and the streetlights illuminate its face, giving the features a yellow-orange glow.

"Do you know him?" says Gibb.

Iris touches her fist to the forehead, middle finger raised.

Her father is leaner than she remembers. Greyer too. His leather coat looks new. He's sharp and handsome and Iris sees him as Mrs. B probably does, maybe even as her mother saw him once upon a time. Beware men in uniform. A leather coat isn't army greens but it can still fool the eye. It's been almost a year since Iris has seen him in person. He tends to travel for work, which is probably why he here.

The three of them stand around the stairs. Iris is forced to bring out her phone. Despite having years to learn, her father only knows a few words in sign language. Growing up, Justine and Iris capitalized on this fault by having secret conversations in plain sight. They had hoped to shame him, and it had worked; one night, maddened by Justine's refusal to stop, he tied her hands behind her back. Now he shuffles in place, glaring at Gibb, but Iris recognizes the same menace behind those cool green eyes. Both these men have ambushed her tonight, but at least Gibb is self-aware. Her father would never wonder if *his* behavior was stalker-ish. He always does as he likes.

"Got in this morning," says Ellington Cook. "Here 'til Friday."

"What is it you do, Mr. Cook?" asks Gibb.

"Sales." Ellington waves his hand in dismissal. Gibb won't get anything else out of him. Even Iris can't say for certain what her father does. He's been an itinerant since the paper company closed. Justine believes he's always breaking the law. She calls him Ellington *Crook*.

"You her boyfriend?"

"We're having a sort-of date."

"Either have a date or don't have one," said Ellington. "Honestly. What's with young people?"

All this time, Iris has been typing a lengthy message asking her father why he's here. Not here-as-in-Montreal but here-as-in-sitting-on-her-stoop-at-eleven-thirty-at-night. After reading the message, Ellington asks why he needs a reason to see his daughter and Iris reminds him that they aren't the sort for random reunions and Ellington growls and Gibb suggests that he let them go inside to talk and Iris takes his sleeve and pulls him back.

"Scared to spend five minutes with me?" Ellington rolls his eyes. "That's her sister's doing."

Iris exhales, blowing air through her nose. *Text me tomorrow*, she writes. *We'll talk then.* She turns to Gibb, points to him, then to herself, then up to the apartment. Gibb nods in understanding and tries to escort her up the stairs. But Ellington reaches out and grabs Iris by the arm.

"Marta found your sister at the house. Justine is packing things up. She's *stealing* from me." Her father can't sign but he can read Iris' face—that face that never shuts up. Her expression gives her away. "I was going to ask you to talk sense into her. But I guess you knew about it, didn't you?"

His grip grows tight. Her attention is on her father, but Iris can feel Gibb behind her, the cavalry guarding her flank. She puts her hand on her father's and pries each finger loose.

"Don't ever have daughters," he says to Gibb. "They don't know loyalty. Women stick to their own. The wedding's coming up. Marta's children are coming from all over the world. Meanwhile, my daughters won't return a text." At least he turns back to Iris. "I'm coming up. We're going to talk about this. *Alone.*"

He grabs Iris again and tries to guide her towards the apartment. His breath is a whiskey-drenched puff in the cold night. Gibb tries to intervene, and Ellington gives him a quarterback's shove, knocking him into the rail. Still holding Iris with one hand, he grabs Gibb's collar by the other and tells the sort-of date that it's time to leave. But he's distracted himself and this gives Iris the chance she needs. She also has one arm free—it's the one carrying her clarinet. Swinging it around, she clips the side of her father's head. Ellington lets out a yelp and releases her, allowing her to grab a large chunk of that leather coat and yank him away from Gibb with such force that she hears something tear. Gibb holds his mouth—somehow, his lip was cut and now there's blood on his chin. This flips the switch. Justine isn't the only angry daughter of Ellington Cook. Using the clarinet case as a prod, Iris pushes her father away from the stoop. Then she lays into him. Since she's holding the clarinet case, she often mouths the words or lets her free hand do the yelling. Her father stares at her with an agitated look, not understanding, unable to read her lips let alone her signs. At last, he grabs her wrist to silence her. It's as bad as forcing a gag in her mouth and Gibb returns to the fray. Breaking Ellington's grip, he shields Iris with his body and gives her a chance to retreat. Ellington lunges again but this time Gibb is a wall that knocks Ellington back. Then he follows Iris up the steps. At first, it's a horror movie scene—she can't get find the key—but when she looks back, she sees her father languishing at the bottom of the stairs. Having fallen again, he's landed in a humiliating flourish and she wishes she had time to take a picture for Justine, for the internet, for the world. He's a heap, a pile of withered leaves.

In the bathroom, Iris washes Gibb's face and applies antiseptic to the cut. Just a scratch, likely from the edge of Ellington's watch.

He tells her she's a good nurse but a better soldier. If he's ever in another ambush, he wants her in his squad. She can smell his great masculine musk, the soldier coming out of heat.

He leaves to check if Ellington is still lurking outside. Iris splashes water on her face and the waterdrops quiver on her hands. Gibb calls out: Ellington is gone. But not silent. Sliding out of airplane mode, her phone hums as it gathers a new string of angry texts. Ignoring them, Iris sends a warning message to Justine. It wouldn't be beyond their father to call the town cops, even if it only gives Justine a hard time. Who knows? He might try to ambush her in Toronto. Justine needs to be ready. Glimpsing her own reflection, Iris thinks she looks wild and a little fierce. She can see the spark in her eyes even as it dwindles away.

In the other room, Gibb is still stationed by the window, not quite sure if he's guard or guest. Her clarinet case is on the table and she snaps it open.

"Did she survive?" asks Gibb.

Iris inspects each piece before assembling the instrument, pressing on each key to make sure they haven't come loose. Gibb stays back. She has a surgeon's concentration and he seems to know not to interfere.

"That woman he's marrying?" says Gibb. "Does she know what he's like?"

Iris shrugs as she slips the clarinet's bell into place.

"Most of the guys I'm with, they all have their pasts. We're not supposed to ask too much about that either. So, we're fighting a war we're not supposed to question and relying on people we know nothing about." He considers her as she wets the reed. "Probably not much you can do. Even if you tried telling her. Nothing good ever comes from getting between a person and their fairy tale."

Iris glances up, cocking an eyebrow.

"Let's say Diedre has a habit of choosing the wrong men." He taps his chin, touching the bandage which Iris has affixed with care. "You want to tell me what you were saying out there to him?"

Nothing, signs Iris. *Everything*. She knows he doesn't understand. God, why are there are always so many words? She finishes fixing the reed to the mouthpiece and puts it to her lips. It's late but the walls are thick, and her neighbors have never complained, even when she's played after midnight. Now the clarinet sings. At first, the voice trembles because of her hands but the muscles soon assert control. The sound is pure; the instrument survived its brief stint as a weapon of minor destruction. Iris doesn't play the Gershwin medley. This is an original. An improvisation. No. A chatter. She meets Gibb's gaze and tries to push her thoughts into the world. Don't go to Afghanistan. The adventure will be here. He's all smiles but she doesn't quite see the flash of understanding. In rehearsals, Professor Wells told the actors that all characters want something. They talk to get it and when that doesn't work, they sing. And when that fails, there's only dance. Damn it, thinks Iris, the sea witch wasn't entirely wrong. Sometimes body language is all that's left.

She stops playing and goes to him, clarinet in hand. This is what it takes to roller-skate through traffic. Struck down, Gershwin barreled on. Iris has never initiated a kiss, but she loves the feeling of it, the power that comes from controlling the moment, shaping the narrative, making the evening her own. And the pleasure that comes from having the gesture returned! (#kisstheboy.) On the couch, they continue to talk in touches and hints. Her roommate, were she home, would have heard nothing but the rustle of clothes when, in fact, there is a whole conversation, a gentle negotiation of the terrain by two new explorers who are still trying to figure out what's right. For the moment, it works. Gibb doesn't have to ask to spend the night and Iris doesn't have to issue the invitation; they just go to bed and he stays.

THE BINDING

JO'VAN O'NEAL

I lay my once coveted head for all my fathers and still, none
notice the sultry of my neck. The way I crook to convince

my body of the familiar. Instead, I become a map to praise.

A rabid necked Nigga. I am all the things the blade required. Here
the milk of my name falls out my hollow face. In another world

this is the taxonomy of suffering. Every son after me is nursing

of lamb and limb. Lineage to nothing. Patron saint for all the boys.
I am. Did they even ask? If they had, my bodies would all sing *no*

in unison. First boy without a prayer. Here I am. Quiet. Choired chaos.

No one thinks of the rammed til they want to be warm or full. Men
wouldn't dare whisper my name in place of their shared gods. Ain't I gift

a century's promise.

Why my neck?
Why my neck?
Why my neck?

I Am Not Still in the Night

Camille Lowry

I am fighting so hard right now. I'm fighting to hold on to my face, my hands and my mind. Anxiety is my opponent. It's not a new foe. But it's grown mighty in the last eight months. I've grown, too—grown more nervous, vigilant, and fearful.

When asked by my mother, father, sister, old friend, dear neighbor, family doctor, therapist, why I'm so afraid, so anxious, I can give many answers, and all of them would make sense to the most practical, positive, and sound minds. I have been suffering from sustained injuries. There have been major muscle strains that continue to require physical therapy. In that fragile state, I was hit by a car as a pedestrian. After that I got whiplash in another accident. I suffered an allergic reaction to something that left my skin itchy and raw for a week, and on and on. Chinese water torture of regular insults to my body. Micro traumas over eight months that have merged to just a general feeling of trauma I can't quite shake.

I could explain all of that. Instead, the first answer that rises up is that I am scared that I am buckling under the anxiety and I will never free myself of it.

This is frightening because I have never been a fatalist, a give-up-er. My brain has been in a loop searching for a way back, wondering who might know best, and mourning the bits of me this strain has cost me.

Years ago I was fitted for a mouth guard for teeth clenching, an aging ritual many adults I know have gone through. The guard is a barrier against damage, worn teeth and lockjaw, but it does not undo the physical habit of biting down. I don't want a shield from the anxiety; I want it slayed.

At times I've wondered if the solution, the lesson to learn, is to just surrender to the anxiety, not try to fight against it. I have stood with my bare feet on my hardwood floors trying to feel strong and stable, and said out loud, "I surrender." Yelling out to the ceiling, to the curtains, to the framed art on the walls, to the dust bunnies gathering in the corners, to no one but myself. Hoping that my mind will feel a little lighter, and that without the fight there will be more space for peace, or at least, for the old, calmer parts of me.

That has not worked. Most mornings I find that my hands are numb and tingling from having clenched all night. Many nights I have curled up into a fetal position, pushing those fists up and into my face. I wake and find bruises on my cheekbones, nail marks besides my eyes, a scratch above my eyebrow, the texture of my forehead bumpy and unrecognizable to me, fight or flight stress hormones roiling it from once butter-smooth to weathered and tough. The wounds are subtle, more painful to feel than visible to others. But I mourn each mark over coffee in the morning after giving myself one look in the mirror, and then I stay away.

I have other rituals. Meditations, journaling and lists of gratitude for what is good in my life, saying no to invitations so I can just sit still and do nothing, claiming time instead for rest. I present my skin to the puncture of the needles of the acupuncturist. I drink less wine and eat more CBD. A nightly scooping of magnesium into warm water and guzzling the minerals down my throat. There have been discussions of perhaps taking something stronger, and which thing over another, and whether the side effects will bring on more worry.

I have gotten down on my knees on my white sheepskin rug beside my bed and prayed for the night habits to go away, even though I am not religious. I spend the next few minutes hoping I won't be physically punished more for being a heathen and a hypocrite.

We, my team of healers, family, and concerned loved ones, theorize on remedies. They assure me that there will be a solution. I try to take comfort in that. But then I wonder, what kind of shape will I be in by the time we do? Will my hands be riddled with arthritis from the blood flow being cut off for months? Will my face be permanently mottled, my disposition always set a little on an edgy tilt?

I had not reacted this way to anxiety before the last four months. I had just been your average kvetching neurotic, verbally wringing my hands. I was an occasional insomniac, waking at four a.m. to worry about past mistakes and if I'd paid my insurance bill. Ironically, now I sleep through the night; I just rough myself while I do it.

I do not think that anything that has happened to me recently warrants such a reaction. What does my body think it is doing? Are the curled fists to protect me against the terrors in my subconscious? Or is my body raging, angry at not having found love or a companion to hold me and say you will be okay? Raging at not having made a family, found my purpose? Am I angry at swallowing hurt feelings, the injustice and doom I read in the news, feeling powerless against it all? I am not sure. I just want it to stop.

I can say that I am angry that no one can tell me with certainty how to fix it.

I keep being encouraged to let out my feelings. "Scream when you drive on the highway," suggested my brother. The screams have not felt natural, but the tears have begun.

A masseuse, which a concerned friend treated me to, came to my house and set up a firm massage bed right in my living room. I lay in a space usually just used as an entryway, floating beside the couch. Unlike in most massages, she talked nearly the whole time. She spoke to me in quiet soothing tones. She told me she was an intuitive empath. As she rubbed my sore hands, she said, "Let it out," and soon I was crying before this complete stranger. Tears have also rolled from my eyes as I pointed out all the parts that pained me to my acupuncturist.

"Maybe I need an exorcism," I started to joke to friends. This being LA, people didn't laugh back, but instead started emailing me sincere referrals to energy healers.

I would have previously rolled my eyes at this idea. Seeing an energy healer is not the kind of thing I was raised to do. My mother thinks taking a Tums will fix any physical condition, that and a glass of wine or two. She goes to the movies to take her mind off troubles. She doesn't believe in preventative self-care like sunscreen. The mention of meditation or any kind of spirituality makes her say, "Oh please." Her version of "phooey."

Despite my family-taught cynicism, I gathered a list of four shamans, and the number of a hypnotist to boot. Based on a suggestion from the friend who has similar nerves to mine, who is also not into anything too woo-woo groovy, I chose a healer and booked an appointment. Under her care, she told me,

"Feel the fear," and soon I was sobbing, my face folding into itself with grief, as tight as my hands do at night.

I had never thought I was one to hide thoughts or feelings. I, who have no poker face, who journals daily, who when feeling troubled, will quickly choose the option Regis Philbin offered—call a friend. I am an essayist and a memoirist who works to make art by examining my past and emotions. I am a let-it-all-hang-out kind of person. If anything, I'm an over-sharer.

I find it unbelievable that somehow I might still have so many more feelings tucked inside that they wage war against me in my sleep. Most nights I have benign dreams that give no sign of hidden internal terror. At worst there are frustration dreams of travel and not being able to get to a gate on time. Yet, something so powerful is surging inside my brain that even if I barricade my face with pillows, my hands find their way beneath the cushions and press into my skin. I do not feel them moving in my sleep. I wake to pain of their pressure, and a panic that it has happened again.

When I was a child I saw snippets from a Michael Caine murder movie called The Hand. I only saw the preview. I was too young to be let into the theater when it was released, and I would have been scared to watch the whole movie anyway. I have never forgotten the few images I saw. Caine's hand is severed in a car accident. The hand lives on, haunted and violent.

I now feel like my life is a mash up of *The Hand* and *Broadcast News*. I have become the Holly Hunter character. During the day I am full of enterprise and industry, discipline and high function, as she was when playing the news producer role. And like Holly, I have a full-out daily cry. Unfortunately, I do not feel as relieved by the release of tears as Holly seemed to—at least, not yet. I feel haunted like Caine, who was trying to outrun a piece of himself.

What I do know is that with all of the appointments made, consultations, fees, brainstorming, soul searching and time spent to find peace, I will have done the work, the hard work of facing what ails me. I will have faced the fear alone in the dark of night. It has been exhausting. But surely something healing must come of it.

I want to think there is a reason things happen, the whole greater purpose thing. I want to think the gift, when this trial ends, will be a deeper knowledge of how the body and spirit can be resilient. That I will know how to turn off the panic and soothe myself easier, faster, and hear the wail that starts to rise inside, long before it grips me.

Self-Portrait as Perdita in 33 Washes of Purple

Dayna Patterson

in the matrix of mother's womb / matter doubled and bloomed till I grew

Royal   Imperial   Bohemian

ousted from her ocean / *queen of curds and cream* / nursed by a stone

Thistle   Wisteria   Lilac

locked up in postpartum asylum / I wanted to wind back Time / beg

Eggplant   Byzantium   Plum

her blessing / bring balm and passage / out of the flooded town / its

Phlox   Veronica   Mallow

moldy bruise I'd / travel with flax / stitch the split / her from herself

Heather   Violet   Pansy

her from us couldn't keep / *this dream of mine* whole / green gone to muck

Puce   Purpureus   Mountbatten

being now awake / cistern to cesspit / *I'll queen it no inch farther, but milk*

Pale   Damson   Eminence

and weep / at market I'd sidle up to strangers / cling *O lady Fortune* to a past

Clematis   Twilight   Orchid

past redeeming only / reckoning left I seek / to undo this tangle / umbilical

Dark   Antique   Tyrian

legacy to pestle / pied as winter's gillyvors / would bone thicken / scaffold

Hot Lavender   Flower-de-luce   Mauve

different if she'd / rooted her feet / anchored deep / sewn a thawing

Mother-of-Pearl   Opal   Heliotrope

dress of spring / not stranded / abandoned / a beach awash in / if / if / if

WATER WARS

SHINELLE L. ESPAILLAT

Week One

The wars began in the main conference room on a Tuesday in November, on the second floor of the GenComm facility in Westchester County, NY. We shuffled our shoes over the plush gray carpet, sustainable water bottles in hand, expecting a two-hour meeting dissecting everything we'd done wrong at the last presentation. We found the Director and an HR tribunal standing at the far end of the room.

The Director, tall and bloated, waved us into our seats around the mahogany table. His chin melted into his neck, and his skin seemed always to have been freshly stretched over his cheeks and left to sag into the folds of his jowls. No one knew what color his eyes were, as he always had them narrowed in suspicious disapproval.

Trevor sat three seats down from the director—close enough to be paying visible attention, but far enough to surreptitiously text. Winnie sat directly across from Trevor. We all suspected that they had a thing going on, but nobody had any proof. Frieda dropped heavily into a chair by the Director, sighing with the expulsion of so much energy. Bob from Accounting and I sat on either side of little Brynn, who always smiled and never minded that people thought of and called her little Brynn, even though we thought she might be at least thirty.

The HR tribunal, blue-suited and silent, stood in the shadowed space behind the director, arms behind their backs, faces stoic and stern. Two of them fanned out slightly from the point where the third stood, so that they formed a kind of arrow, pointing at the Director. He took his seat at the head of the table and pushed back his chair, so that he stared at us over the mass of his belly. His squinting eyes and compressed lips made some of us feel as though we'd done something wrong.

"Well." He let the word hang in the air for a moment. "I have to tell you, it has not been a good year. We need to make some adjustments, cutbacks."

All our heads snapped toward him. Trevor's thumb froze mid-text. The Director said nothing, let the impressive silence bounce off the white walls. Kyla rolled her eyes. One of the HR tribunal cleared her throat.

"You were going to explain about the cutbacks?" The other two cleared their throats as well.

"Yes. So what I have to share is that there isn't going to be any more water."

We waited. He didn't seem inclined to elaborate.

Kyla asked what we'd all been thinking. "What do you mean, there isn't going to be any more water? What—on Earth?"

The Director frowned. "In the building."

"I'm sorry. I don't understand. How can there not be any more water in the building? That just doesn't make any sense."

He flapped his hands dismissively at her. "I don't understand what you don't understand. Cutbacks. You'll have to bring your own water from home."

"You mean you're getting rid of the coolers?" Trevor's face, always pale against his blond hair, turned whiter. He was one who refilled his bottle at least three times a day. He said he had a condition.

The Director sniffed. "All the water. Coolers, sinks, toilets. You'll have to bring it from home. Cutbacks. Now. We need to discuss that last presentation. Atrocious."

"Wait a minute, Sir." Kyla managed to throw a world of contempt into that "sir." "You cannot fail to provide water in the toilets. That has to be some kind of health code violation."

He smiled at her. "Prove it."

"Look." The woman from the HR tribunal glared at the Director as though she would like to slice through him. "It is possible that this will merely be temporary. But we must take strong measures to get the budget back on track. The plumbing will still work; you will just have to provide your own water to facilitate it. We are not telling you that you cannot drink water on-site. I fail to see the problem. Unless you would prefer that we cut salaries instead. Or positions."

No one had a ready response. We could see uniformed delivery men wheeling the coolers past the conference room doors. We stared at each other, aghast. Since the redistricting, none of us who lived below Rye had drinkable water at home. We joked that the government must think that the lower property values and rent meant you could afford to buy bottles. The tinged, textured water that came up to lower Westchester wasn't exactly pleasant for bathing either, but we made do, taking quick showers with scented soap, brushing our teeth with bottled water, and knowing that we could have clear, clean water at work. Frieda, breathing heavily, held a hand to her throat, as though she were already burning with thirst. Winnie clutched her bottle close, taking small, quick sips. Trevor's thumbs worked double time under the table.

The Director smirked and nodded. "That last presentation. Atrocious."

Week Two

Kyla filed a claim with OSHA, but hadn't heard anything back yet. On Tuesday, someone mugged little Brynn. Just like the rest of us, she had started each day by lugging a few Stop & Shop gallon jugs of water through the parking lot. If I happened to get there at the same time, I would usually try to help her, even though I had my own load to carry. Twice, though, I just sat in my car and pretended not to see her zig-zagging under the weight of her burdens. Mine were heavy enough on their own. She got in early that day, before the sun had fully dispelled the dark chill. Someone snatched two of her gallons and knocked her over. She'd curled in a fetal position around the last one, crying for help. When I got there, Bob from Accounting was standing by her, his car blocking the lot. He said he'd nearly run over her.

She wouldn't let go of her last jug, and she wouldn't get off the ground. We had to leave our jugs in our trunks and carry her inside. Frieda gasped, barreled down the hallway and knocked me aside, snatching little Brynn into her arms.

"Oh my Gawd, what happened to her" Frieda glared at me. I raised my hands, palms outward, and used my soft voice.

"I have no idea."

"Hey, we just helped her—we found her like that!" Bob from Accounting had a deep, booming voice that carried through cubicle walls and closed doors alike. "We don't know who did this. Didn't you see her when you got in? Why didn't *you* help her?"

Frieda's nasal squawk competed with his megaphone bass. Little Brynn stood there shaking, arms wrapped around the jug, until Frieda shushed him and got little Brynn to say what happened. Winnie started crying.

Kyla stood with her hands on her hips. "Did you get a look at the guy? Maybe we can try to catch him." I appreciated her practicality, and the fact that she didn't assume it was me. "We can't just let a predator roam around the building." Winnie's sobs grew louder. Kyla rolled her eyes and handed her a tissue.

"How do you know it was a 'him'?" Trevor shifted from one foot to another. "I mean, it could have been anybody, right?"

It was certainly true that a strong wind could have knocked over little Brynn, but everyone had been giving Trevor a quiet side-eye since the big announcement. He was always thirsty, always out of his own water and borrowing from someone else. He kept reminding us that he had a condition. I noticed that his sustainable bottle was full. Bob from Accounting nudged me and nodded his head toward Trevor's bottle, but neither of us said anything. Frieda offered to keep little Brynn's last gallon locked in the filing cabinet with her own. Bob from Accounting and I went back out to the parking lot to get our own bottles. It seemed like it was going to be a rough day.

By Friday, we'd gone from not trusting Trevor to not trusting anyone. HR had issued a memo stating their intent to find and prosecute the "person or persons responsible for the assault and water theft," and reminding us that this was probably temporary and that we should continue to shoulder responsibility for our own drinking/handwashing/flushing situations. Little Brynn announced that she had applied for a gun permit, and kept updating anyone within hearing about the status. She didn't smile anymore. Winnie tightened her grip on her bottle any time I walked past her cubicle. Nobody wanted to use the bathroom after Bob from Accounting, who blatantly refused to shoulder responsibility for his own flushing situation, even after the Director had told him that failure to do so might come up in his next review. Frieda gave up all pretense of working, and sat guard in front of her filing cabinet, arms crossed, head turning slowly from one shoulder to another as she did a careful sweep of the hallway. She only left her post for a half hour lunch break. When she came back on Friday and checked her stash, she let out a shriek that shook the walls.

"No! Oh my Gawd! Who did this?" Half of us had rushed to the hall at her first scream, and her wild eyes accused us each in turn. "Was it you? Was it you?"

"Frieda, nobody knows what you're talking about. What happened?" Kyla's voice was calm and soothing. But of course, we knew what happened.

"Somebody broke in and stole my last gallon! Who would do that? What kind of animal steals someone else's water? Was it you?" She pointed an accusing finger at me. I held up my hands to show they were empty. She didn't even wait for me to respond. "Was it you?" She pointed at Kyla.

"We all have our own water, Frieda. Nobody needs to steal from you." Kyla didn't even seem bothered by the accusation. Frieda took a breath to accuse someone else, then shrieked again.

"Aha! I know it was YOU!" We followed her blazing eyes and pointing finger down the hall, where Trevor stood, rubbing one foot against the back of the opposite leg, slurping from his sustainable bottle. He froze when he realized we were watching him.

"Wait, what?"

"YOU STOLE MY WATER!"

"I—no!"

"THIEF! ANIMAL! THIEF!" She started charging down the hall toward him. He backed toward the door.

"I have a condition!" He tossed the cup to try to defend himself, but he was too slow, and Frieda ran full force into him. We saw his feet leave the ground, heard his head catch the corner of a metal cabinet. He lay still on the gray carpet. Frieda stood over him, fists clenched, bosom heaving.

The Director came out of his office, looked at Trevor lying blond, pale, and still, and glared at us. "This is a fine kettle of fish."

Week Three

It turned out that Trevor was only severely concussed. Plus, it took fifteen stitches to close his head gash. He was still at Westchester Medical Center on Monday, so Winnie, Kyla, Bob from Accounting and I went to visit. We ran into his mother outside his room. She told us that Trevor really did have a condition: malabsorption syndrome.

We went into the room. Winnie flipped her hair over her shoulder and marched straight to Trevor's side. She ran a hand over his IV bag, and he reached out to pull the pole closer. We could see several empty water bottles on the nightstand next to him. He held a cup of ice, from which he kept pulling a single chunk to crunch.

"Thanks for visiting, guys. I'm in so much pain. I feel terrible."

Bob from Accounting shrugged. "Least you got away from GenComm for a few days. Looks like you got all the water you want here."

Trevor shrugged too. "It's alright, I guess. But the nurses get snippy when you ask them to bring you more water."

Kyla rolled her eyes. "It's not as though they have any other responsibilities, like, I don't know, keeping people alive."

"Hey. Water *is* life." He popped an ice chunk in his mouth and crunched, closing his eyes. Winnie took the opportunity to snatch a chunk herself, holding it in her mouth rather than crunching it.

Bob from Accounting cleared his throat. "Hey Trevor. Just out of curiosity. Were you the one who jacked little Brynn? We won't rat you out. You're among friends." This may or may not have been true. Winnie certainly wouldn't say anything—she never said anything.

Trevor swallowed. He opened his eyes, then widened them and sat up straighter.

"Hello Trevor." Our heads all snapped around at the sound of the Director's voice. He stood just inside the doorway. The blue-suited HR tribunal shadowed him in arrowhead formation. "I trust this is a good time?"

"Um. Sir?"

"Well. We needed to see for ourselves your okay-ness." He stepped further into the room. Trevor drew back into his pillows. I wondered how any of them could possibly have time to be there. Who was back at the office doing the work, or at least checking to be sure that Frieda hadn't turned on little Brynn? The woman stepped around the Director and dropped a manila folder on Trevor's lap.

"Please note that as you were not harmed in the course of fulfilling your proscribed duties, you will not qualify for worker's compensation. You must therefore use accumulated sick time for your recovery. If you will miss more than three days of the standard work week, you must submit documentation detailing your injury and explaining why you are unable to return to work, along with supporting medical proof. Failure to do so will be grounds for termination." She turned to look at the rest of us. "Please note this out-of-office time on your timesheets. You must charge these hours to your accumulated vacation time. If you do not have sufficient vacation time, you will not be compensated." The tribunal turned as a unit and left, with the Director trailing after them.

"Well damn," Bob from Accounting said. The only other sound was Trevor and Winnie crunching ice. We left pretty soon after that. Winnie didn't have any accumulated vacation time.

We thought Frieda would be arrested, or at least fired, but she was still in the office every day and still sat guarding her file cabinet of water, only now she didn't leave for lunch; little Brynn just brought her a cheese sandwich from the cafeteria. Kyla said she personally had called the police, and they told her that they were aware that there had been an incident, and that they could not comment on an ongoing investigation. I admired her energy. She could not understand why everyone was accepting what was happening, and she cornered me and Bob from Accounting while we were huddled by the empty water coolers, sipping from our sustainable bottles.

"Literally everything that's happening is criminal—how can you sit back and do nothing?"

Bob from Accounting shrugged. "I mean, it's just easier to roll with it. Honestly, I'm surprised you're kicking up such a fuss. I figured the two of you were used to this kind of stuff. There's water shortages and famines and junk like that all the time where you're from, right?"

I stopped sipping. It took me a second to realize that he was assuming that Kyla and I were both from a non-American, third-world country—the same non-American, third-world country. My name is John Smith. I'm from the Bronx. I wanted to look at Kyla to see her reaction, but I wanted to not look at Kyla so that we wouldn't be having a collective reaction instead of reacting as individuals. But not looking at her was also disassociating myself from her, which I did not want to do. So I turned to her, but she was staring at Bob from Accounting, and all the fire and fury of the universe sparked in her eyes.

"I'm from Chappaqua!" Kyla shouted. No wonder she had been so outraged; she had the good water at home. She stared at him, and he stared back. Then he shrugged and returned to his sustainable bottle. "You know what? I don't have to be here. I don't need this." She turned and left. Bob from Accounting shrugged again, and opened his mouth, but I didn't want to hear him speak. I walked away and caught up to Kyla, who did not slow her pace.

"Can you believe him?" I'd thought Bob from Accounting was cool, and my whole soul was smarting. I wanted her to slow down so we could share our outrage. She did not.

"Yes of course I can believe it. I'm angry, but I'm not shocked. I can see why you're surprised though." She shook her head.

"What does that mean?" I *was* surprised. Didn't I have a right to be?

She turned into her office and started pulling out her coat and purse. "It means that you thought when they said 'we' and 'us' that they always also meant you. I knew that sometimes 'we' meant 'us but not you.' You drank the Kool-aid." She picked up her bag and started walking again. "So what are you going to do now?"

"I don't know. File a complaint with HR, I guess. I know it won't make much difference; I don't think there's anything they can actually do, but at least it'll be on record."

She stopped and looked at me. "Really John? You're going to file a report that someone said something racist with the same HR that just told you that you're not entitled to have water? You're *still* drinking the Kool-aid. I hope that works out for you." She took off again.

"Well what are *you* going to do?" I was getting frustrated. She'd been the one filing reports everywhere, and now that I wanted to file one, she told me that was delusional. I couldn't keep up with her.

"I'm leaving."

"It's the middle of the day! You don't think the Director will notice?"

"I'm not leaving for the day; I'm *leaving*. I got an offer from WestComm—better title, higher salary. I do not need this place. I started shopping my resume the minute they made that clown Director. I could see the writing on the wall."

I followed her outside. "Congratulations. Did you even give notice? You're kind of burning a bridge here."

She snorted. "You keep talking to me as though I should care about this place. Do you really think they don't have money in the budget for *water*? That's crazy! If I didn't live in Chappaqua I'd probably have turned psycho like Frieda."

"Well, not all of us have the luxury of living in Chappaqua! I bet some sorority sister got you the job at WestComm—good for you, but they didn't have Greek life at my college, so I'm kind of on my own." I hadn't realized I was so angry, and maybe I hadn't been until right then. "Why don't you use all those AKA connections to help the rest of us?"

"Delta. Crimson and cream, not green and pink. Believe me, there's a difference. And why are you out here yelling at me when you couldn't say a word to damn Bob?"

I didn't want to answer. I had a feeling she knew my truth better than I did anyway. She looked at me and sighed. "John. For real. You don't have to stay where you are. Get to where the good water is." We made it to the parking lot. She disarmed her Saab and opened the door.

"So that's it, you're just leaving? If you know so much about change, why don't you stay and help?"

"I tried. Nobody would listen. And now it's not my fight anymore. Good luck filing your report." She got in and closed the door. Then she lowered the window. "That wasn't meant to be sarcastic, John. Good luck. You're going to need it." She drove away. I stood there, coatless and shivering. There was no one on my side in this war; no one even knew who or what we were fighting, except thirst. *Water, water everywhere, and not a drop to drink*, I thought. The clouds rolled, heavy, through the sky, but did not release their promised rain. I went back inside to warm up, and to defend my gallons.

WHAT TO DO WITH THE PLANTS
LEAH DIETERICH

Thank you for agreeing to water the plants while we're away. I probably should've asked you to house sit, but I think I need to get to know you better before I'd feel comfortable with you being alone in my house. Anyway, I only need you to water the plants outside. There are a few inside, but I'm seeing how long it takes them to die. It's a game we play.

There's a hose coiled by the front door that will stretch all the way down the stairs to the street. Use it to hit those couple of plants growing in the rocks by the curb. One is a Crown of Thorns (I wouldn't have chosen such a Jesus-y plant, but my gardener put it in without asking). I don't know what the others are called. They're kind of aloe-ish. You'll have to use the hose on the other side of the house to water the rest. It's annoying that one hose won't reach all of them, but that's sort of how life is.

Water the cherry tomatoes, eggplant, lettuce, and cucumbers in the tall raised garden boxes against the back of the house. Really soak 'em. You might not want to water in sandals because I've seen black widows there.

If you go up the stairs to the second tier, you'll see a giant raised bed which is empty and dry. Nothing to water there. We had a great crop the first year, but the second year nothing grew. Not even the easy stuff like basil and zucchini. We pulled it all out, thinking we'd try some fall vegetables but as we turned the soil, we found roots so thick and woody we thought they were sticks an animal had buried. Our gardener said they were roots from a tree ten feet away. Seems like a lot of effort for that tree, and for what? Just a power move, I guess.

On the wall behind the sofa, there are five yellow-green agave plants. These don't actually need to be watered either because the sprinklers reach them, but the one thing I always do whenever I walk by them is grab the big cone in the center, down by the base, and close my hand around it. You wanna get a good grip and then pull your closed hand up toward the tip of the cone, allowing your hand to tighten as the circumference of the cone gets smaller. Pay attention to the feeling on your palm and fingers. If you've ever wrapped your hand lightly around a cat's tale and then kept it there as the cat walks away, you know the feeling I'm talking about.

Did I tell you about the time my boyfriend found a disemboweled dog in the yard? Bloody tufts of white fur everywhere. It was like the coyote was aiming for maximum impact. *I'm gonna eat this particular dog because the contrast of the red blood on the white fur will make sure they really notice and are appropriately traumatized. I want them to know that this is not their yard.*

The fig tree at the top of the hill is actually in the neighbor's yard. Some of the branches extend into ours and give us more figs than we know what to do with. The soil up there is almost completely clay so it's a feat to get the figs without caking your shoes or slipping and falling, but you should try. For best results, do it barefoot and just let your feet sink into the clay. (Do this at the end after you've watered the area with the black widows, of course.)

Water the base of the lemon tree next to the fig and take as many lemons as you like. You'll know they're ready if they're not too difficult to pull off. Sometimes there are good ones on the ground too. If while picking up fallen lemons, you accidentally stick your finger right into a soft rotten part, don't be alarmed. It happens to me all the time. At first it feels gross, but hang in there, don't pull your finger out right away. It might make you uncomfortable to be standing in my yard with your finger inside a rotten lemon up past the second knuckle but sit with that feeling. It's good to be uncomfortable. Hold the lemon on your finger up in the air and pretend you're spinning a basketball if it makes you feel better. Once you do take your finger out, it'll smell good. And having a good smelling finger is never a bad thing.

Before you leave, water the succulents at the bottom of the stairs. One of them is wavy like a sea fan and has a thin stalk growing up from the center with little leaves that look like red fingernails, except they're not thin or brittle. Pinch one and you'll see. It's got a pleasing thickness to it. Imagine you're pinching someone's earlobe. You can imagine it's my earlobe if you like, even though mine don't really dangle. They're "attached," as they say. Maybe that's why I'm never single. That's an interesting thing to contemplate: if your earlobes are a predictor of your relationship status. Anyway, pluck five of these earlobe-leaves and carry them back up to the big blue agaves at the very top of the hill. These agave are more dangerous than the yellow-green ones. They're rigid and unforgiving and serrated like knives. Pierce two of the earlobes on their needle-sharp tips. Put the other three in your pocket and take them home and forget about them until you do laundry and find them in the bottom of the washer. This is as much water as they need.

STATES OF COMPROMISE

RYAN HARPER

The Observer: Winter

In southeast Missouri, in northeastern Cape Girardeau County, bordered to the east by the Mississippi River, there is a tract of land called Lovejoy. It was an experiment in Reconstruction. In 1866, a number of black and white men pooled resources to construct a "manual labor school" for freedmen—and, notably, freedwomen. An intentional work-study community, Lovejoy would be a place where African Americans would receive an education as they built and maintained adjacent properties, cultivating the land with and alongside each other, in a riverside location auspicious for enterprise and industry. Pennsylvania Quaker Wilmer Walton spearheaded the effort. For the next decade, Walton would live, work, and teach in Lovejoy, the only white resident in the community.

River pilots call it Lovejoy Landing. Located at a slight crook in the river, just north of the more prominent Neely's Landing, Lovejoy Landing is not a working port, but a natural aid to navigation for workers on the big public waters. Lovejoy is now private property—rough, forested terrain, no public roads in or out. I lived the first two decades of my life just a few miles from the place, but I had not heard of it until a recent conversation with my friend, local historian Denise Lincoln. A long-time Cape Girardeau citizen, Denise has spent her late middle age doing tireless archival work, tracking down the hidden stories of African Americans who lived in nineteenth century southeast Missouri. "Check Google Maps; it's there," she told me with a grin, invoking the contemporary online rite of final confirmation. A Missourian in full, Denise is well-apprised of maps and legends. Google had heard of Lovejoy. How hadn't I heard?

Fourteen hundred miles away, in central Maine, in northeastern Kennebec County, which is divided by the Kennebec River, I walk to work up Mayflower Hill, in the city of Waterville. It is January 2020, the middle of my second year teaching at Colby College. The snowmelt saddens me. The temperature broke fifty degrees Fahrenheit yesterday. What little snow we have accumulated this year has thawed into a porridge of sand and cinder. Had such a warm spell occurred my first Maine January, I would have experienced it as a grace. But the indisputability of winter here has come to constitute its appeal to me—the clarity of its terms, the equipage, requisite. Uncompromising. How can I have failed to snowshoe this year? I await the dark season's cues, wondering how long it will take to regenerate the pack. Under the scattered light of a dry winter sky I walk.

Elijah Parish Lovejoy graduated from Colby—then Waterville Seminary—in 1826. In the 1830s, the Presbyterian cleric became an abolitionist lightning rod in St. Louis, Missouri, operating a press and running editorials denouncing slavery in his paper, the *St. Louis Observer*. After the slaveholding interests in slave-state Missouri destroyed his press numerous times, Lovejoy set up shop across the river in Alton, Illinois, printing abolitionist articles in his new *Alton Observer*. But border states trade properties. Free-state Illinois possessed its own slaveholding interests. On November 7, 1837, a proslavery mob descended on the warehouse where Lovejoy had been forced to hide his press. Gunfire was exchanged. Two people were killed. One was Lovejoy. For the second time, his press was demolished, cast into the Mississippi River. His life and death caused the Lovejoy name to appear wherever people championed the free dissemination of ideas and freedom from slavery.

At Colby, my office is on the third floor of Lovejoy Hall.

Two hundred years ago, Missouri and Maine became yoked forever by the conditions of their statehood, a slave region and free region forced to walk arm-in-arm into the United States. Designed to preserve the Union, the Missouri Compromise revealed just how precarious that union was. The Compromise granted white supremacists a seat at the American table of power and, by virtue of the concessions they won, guaranteed them a future seat. The deal involved powerful anti-slavery *interests*, but not enslaved *people*—an extraordinary compromise, that conceded nothing to the population at the center of the debate.

Two hundred years later, I am wondering about what we carry—we who have lived in the states of compromise. It is 2020: a time of quarantine, of enforced and voluntary distance, of the cutting of the breath, the spirit. I am wondering what positions are binding, are fatal, whether we might commute what lines we can.

The Boundary

Missouri borders eight states—tied with Tennessee, more than any other state. Maine borders only one state—the fewest in the lower 48. Maine is a destination, Missouri a gateway, Arch and all. An out-of-state license plate on a Missouri highway signals a driver on her way elsewhere. Excepting occasional Canadians, an out-of-state license plate in Maine signals a trip just begun or just completed. You are in Maine because you live there, or because you came to visit. The gauntlet of welcome signs on Interstate 95 lets you know that Mainers know this:

STATE LINE
Maine
VACATIONLAND

MAINE
WELCOME HOME

Or, when proto-Trump Paul LePage was the state's governor:

WELCOME TO
MAINE
The Way Life Should Be
OPEN FOR BUSINESS

All are posted on rest-stop blue or green metal, in blocky, telegram font, without punctuation marks, pictures, or graphics. It makes for one of the most unceremonious border crossings in the nation. A few miles in, the brown tourist bureau's sign seems downright pornographic by comparison, with the state silhouette in green, the gratuitous use of italics and periods: *Maine. Worth a Visit. Worth a Lifetime.*

The passive-aggressive greeting matches Maine's ambivalent attitude toward itself and to visitors. The state needs money, and, if it must, people. But the state is proudly rural, wooded, and, by East Coast standards, wild. The state will take your money, but it is both poor taste and poor investment to beg by the roadsides. Maine outlawed billboards beginning in 1978 and has shot down every effort to rescind the ban. Even free market maniac LePage did not court business with glitter and fireworks; OPEN FOR BUSINESS was enough. The trees and the water provide their own testimony. If they will not suffice, you may as well turn around; Maine is neither your home nor your vacationland.

The stretch of Missouri interstate I know best—Interstate 55, south of St. Louis to Cape Girardeau—cuts through a lovely stretch of land just west of the Mississippi River valley, just east of the Lead Belt hill country. Farm fields share the hillsides with thick stands of hardwood trees, and occasional stone steeples testify to the region's old German Lutheran and French Catholic populations. The drive from St. Louis to Kansas City on Interstate 70 contains its own potential charm as well, with larger stretches of flatter farmland and bigger sky, the soil rolling at choice moments along the Missouri River basin.

But advertising defiles both roadscapes. The paying culture tells its interests, every magnified jot and tittle, every mile. You will not drive one minute without encountering a billboard for the nearest exit with a McDonald's Playland, a forty-foot Bible verse, a sixty-foot Second Amendment, an all-caps ad for the nearest adult video store, a picture of a fetus, blown up in more-than-full personhood. The fetuses particularly prevail on Interstate 55, a corridor of cobelligerent conservative Christianity: the reigning Lutheranism, Missouri Synod; the Catholicism, magisterial, ultramontane (until a Jesuit assumed the See); every other Christian, a variety of evangelical.

They all hang with you—more so than the ads, say, in midtown New York City. Urban ad density creates a photomosaic—troubling in its own right— but the discrete messages make little impression. In Missouri, there is acreage enough for each billboard to sustain its lurid singularity even as it augments the horrifying whole. At the same time, the obsession with hanging it all so garishly on the highways bespeaks the paying culture's anxious suspicion that, in reality, none of it hangs together, on its own. Nothing can be trusted to bear its own witness. Commuters require counsel: what to buy, what to feel, where to get off.

It makes some sense. In a gateway state, where everyone is passing through, Missourians must make a quick pitch. Like Missouri, Maine has a fierce deregulatory streak, but it does not possess the same relationship with its commuters. Urgency is needless. People are in Maine either because they cannot get out, or because the pitch already has been made, successfully. I felt unmoored when I first moved to the Pine Tree State, to that unsoliciting edge. This was partly due to my having moved from New York City, where I still lived during the "non-academic" portions of the year with my spouse. But that city had unmoored me, too, when I moved there. It was coastal, like Maine. And the relentless solicitation in New York—where everyone had a hustle—had a self-cancelling effect, leaving me feeling as unnecessary as Maine did. I came of age tucked inland, sheltered by the constant commercial and moral attention of the Show Me State's paying culture. I still feel it when I return to Missouri; it can feel as cozy as a warm bed, even for those of us who kick at the blankets—the way a shopping mall can feel homey to even skeptical white people, if we permit the lights and sounds their soft dominion. We know, despite ourselves, it is all for us.

When I first travelled to Waterville, I thought I was driving off the edge of the planet. It was early April, the browning season, when the snow metamorphizes from blessed rule to exception, when even the landscape withdraws its best offer. Turning off the interstate, I realized, alas, civilization had arrived before me. Waterville, population 16,000, somehow sustained two Burger Kings, two McDonalds, I am not certain how many Dunkin' Donuts, and consequently two hospitals. I felt disappointed and relieved. As I spent weekends daring farther northward—to Bangor, to Baxter, even to Presque Isle—the cycle repeated: each horizon would be my last, the cliff was approaching, then I landed, sighing, at the next settlement. To be sure, things get sparse in the north country. But Vacationland is not the ends of the earth.

The Light

We Missourians worshipped the coast as only the landlocked could. *Coastal Living* magazine rivalled the Bible in its ubiquity. Those ultramarine covers, oiled up in bromide, steered us through our every holding pattern, from the grocery check-out line, to the wicker basket adjacent to the living room sofa, to the dentist's waiting room—wherever one prayed for smooth sailing and a numbness that endureth. Our god was not the coast but the idea of the coast: summery, white, and overlit, forever and ever.

The lighthouse was the central icon of this gnostic littoralism. Lighthouses suffer from excess of applicability. Missouri is filled with them. Thomas Kinkade's lighthouse paintings lined the walls of my evangelical friends' homes, sometimes augmented by ceramic lighthouse statuary, or lighthouse table lamps. On occasion, the works included a caption—Bible verses about light shining in the darkness or houses built upon rocks. Usually, the lighthouses stood wordless in a word-tossed world, alongside framed hangings from Hobby Lobby that raged, in faux-embroidered capital letters, "FAITH," "FAMILY," or "BLESS THIS HOUSE." Altar and liturgy, every room instructed visitors on what to feel. Lighthouses were the most subtle symbols we would countenance.

The lighthouse paintings almost always situate the viewer terrestrially— at a distance from the tower sufficient to capture it all, but still on some nearby peninsula, or behind the scene, inland. Missourians do not live near coastal lighthouses, which is perhaps one reason it bothers no one that the genre's common perspective is rare. While Maine's ragged coastline has some stabs of land that provide nice inland views of lighthouses (the light at Portland Head is a popular example), the best views of them usually require crawling out on rocks exposed only during low tides, or taking a ferry. This is no great mystery; lighthouses are built for pilots, in particularly difficult-to-navigate spots. Viewers in unhazardous locales are not a lighthouse's target audience. But evangelical lighthouse art desires the full loveliness of a lighthouse with only implied hazards. Makers of such art rarely provide views from ships, or in the dead of night. Indeed, they rarely depict ships at all. If they do, the vessels appear in the distance, sailing in apparently smooth waters.

Lighthouses present their painters with a paradox: a lighthouse's usefulness is inversely proportional to its visibility. At peak functionality, a lighthouse is only its light. The full body of a lighthouse is visible when it catches and reflects large amounts of external light. Sunny days are the best. A landscape so aglow has no need of artificial illumination, so the tower's light would be off in such a setting, or faint at best, diffused in the luminance of settled weather. One cannot have both the light and the lighthouse.

The best painters of lighthouses know this, and they make a choice. Edward Hopper and Marsden Hartley, both of whom resided in Maine, privilege the structures—trading the extinguished light for the play of shadow on the structure, in landscapes empty with dayglow. British artist William Daniell, in his *Eddystone Lighthouse During a Storm*, opts to show the light, obscuring the structure itself in the black storm, the sea waves. Whether or not they are strict representationalists, genuine painters of light are committed to honesty, which means refusing to lie about the availability of illumination and its juxta-position to darkness. A painter of light must be a painter of darkness. If this is a compromise, it is a compromise rooted in real relation.

But Kinkade and company go in for neither paradox nor compromise. Every light, natural and artificial, is on. They want palpable light with only theoretical darkness—just as they want aids to navigation in a world with only hypothetical hazards. This is why their light fails, as representation and as symbol. An artist cannot sacrifice the ecology of a landscape at the altar of symbolism and expect a symbolism that is anything but kitsch. A compelling symbol is like a compelling theology: it does not come at a discount.

But we Midwesterners bought it. We had our reasons. Maine's grays move; its whites breathe and shimmer. Not colorless, the atmosphere is, in fact, a commuter of color. In Missouri, the grays hung blank, locking the land in with more than land. We lived under season-long tombstone skies—slate in fall and winter, the latter quickly giving way to summers so humid the air was like polished marble. Things cleared and moved in short fits: the time of hail, tornadoes. The skies matched the religious temperament: ashen for much of the year, occasionally kindled by a Pentecostal spark to a ghostly, unforgiving pillar of cloud and fire. We dreamed of another dispensation: a controlled burn, a welcome motion, an abiding, peaceable light. From a distance, we the landlocked sang the idea of the sea.

The Landing

Descended from an extended line of Quakers, Wilmer Walton knew fellowship and disfellowship. The Friends' orthodox faction had disciplined then disowned him in the last years of the Civil War for his inclination toward the Hicksites—the more socially and theologically daring, less well-heeled strand of Quakerism. Before purchasing some Lovejoy property and assuming the role of schoolmaster, fundraiser, and general principal, he had taught freedmen in Alabama, where his progressive pedagogy and egalitarian views rankled his Freedmen's Bureau bosses. Lovejoy would be the restless, homeless Walton's opportunity to attempt a fuller reconstruction.

He and the people of Lovejoy met resistance early. In 1866, a mob burned the schoolhouse down; a literal reconstruction would be one of the community's first projects. Lovejoy's citizens lived under perpetual suspicion that often resulted in threatened and actual violence. Walton was targeted, since area whites regarded him as the sole head of the settlement—an assumption rooted partly in truth, partly in their belief that black people required an autocratic white leader. Walton recorded several instances in which groups of angry white men terrorized him. The worst occurred in 1875, when a masked group that Walton described as a "Ku Klux band" held him at gunpoint, charged him with "teaching niggers," beat him, and let him go with the promise of hanging him if he persisted. The group returned a few nights later to do just that, but were frightened away, according to Walton, "by the presence of a few unarmed colored men" with whom Walton was meeting.

This incident prompted a half-hearted investigation on the parts of local authorities. The conditional, waffling tone of the local press suggests they did not totally believe Walton's report. While they grudgingly admitted Walton was assaulted, they were hesitant to admit Klan presence in southeast Missouri. Had Walton truly been attacked by a racist mob, it had been the work of a handful of slapdash ruffians, whose major crime seemed to be related to "reputation and purse." As Jackson, Missouri's *Cash-Book* newspaper saw it, local authorities had to waste funds on the investigation, and "the thoughtless, lawless act of a few unknown men or boys" made it seem as if the region housed white supremacy of the organized, Klan variety. A few bad eggs caused the entire community to smell rotten.

The tone is as familiar to me as my own name. The high bar for acknowledging white supremacy as a systematic problem is endemic to Missouri, that non-Confederated slave state, from Ferguson to the University of Missouri. Wilmer Walton left Cape County about the same time the Hayes-Tilden Compromise ended Reconstruction. Lovejoy disappeared without report.

The Cape

Cape Girardeau County is landlocked on an edge, on the western banks of the Mississippi. The county seat is the port city of Cape Girardeau: "Cape," everyone calls it. Locals like to declare Cape Girardeau the only inland cape in the nation. The claim's validity depends on one's criteria. True, it is the only inland city called "Cape," but cities with "cape" in their names are rare in the United States, even on coasts. True, there is a significant bend in the river north of town commonly called a cape by the river navigators. However, the rock promontory originally known as "Cape Girardot" was blown up in the 1800s to complete construction of the riverside railroad. Cape was, and is not.

Cape. Not *The Cape.* A childhood friend who attended a private university in St. Louis told me she could tell which of her classmates knew nothing about Missouri if they referred to her home with a definite article: *Are you going back to the Cape this weekend? Isn't it nice to get down to the Cape sometimes?* "The Cape" conjured weekends of highbrow New England leisure: walking the dunes with Elizabeth Bishop by day, drinking with Robert Lowell by night, whiling away the golden hours in softly lit dayrooms and clean-angled houses. "Cape," though, was pool halls, tanning salons, hair product, huge parking lots, and weather too harsh to be poetic because there was no ocean to throw the storms in or out, no marked entries and exits, no stern symmetries.

As a young person in Missouri, I had dreamed of living in New England, though I had not been there. It was my edition of Midwestern littoralism. I had a vague notion that New England was not all coastal, but I believed its proximity to the grumpy Atlantic, that raging, intolerant Puritan, cleansed even the inland recesses of philistine shenanigans. When Missourians travelled to a coast, we went to the placid Gulf of Mexico, usually on the Florida panhandle, which in the summer became one long waterwing warehouse of cracker tackiness. I did not like it. New England, I imagined, housed a life of the mind, fresh-aired literary production, neatly cultivated civic life, surrounded by people who prioritized high thinking and plain but groomed living. I would not have admitted what a pale dream it was—the idea that, somewhere, the right kind of white people lived alone together with their progressive opinions and tastes. Such was life on the Cape.

I quickly learned upon my move to Maine that the state (and the region) had more Cape than *the* Cape. Outside of Mayflower Hill, Waterville and the surrounding area looked more like my Missouri reality than my Missouri dream of New England. I ended up being somewhat glad of this. The intervening years had soured me a good deal on respectable, high society white America. It started before Trump's election, but it escalated afterward, when it became evident that Trump provided self-identifying white progressives of a certain class easy cover for our questionable life choices. Everyone who did not vote for Trump was suddenly in the resistance, and all of our deeds, from selecting wine to visiting the dog park, we decided were courageous. As we always do, entitled white people collapsed and coopted discourses of self-cultivation and self-care to justify all of our consumptive habits—the costs of which are the reason most of the world requires some self-care in the first place. It was quite visible in New York City among people in my demographic, which is probably why I inclined toward the older populations of Harlem, Morningside Heights, and that triple-digit-street portion of the Upper West Side. So too I took to the Mainers beyond Mayflower. I liked their unadorned grit, their cheerless friendliness, their flat-footed clomp through the world. *Cape*, not *The Cape*.

Cape is no more romantic than *The Cape*. The racism of this population is real; it is not total, but it is too total to ignore. The toxic masculinity is real— the guns, the mufflerless pickups, the raging, wheezing report of men who wear only the masks they were given as boys, who feel the very air would be theirs were they strong enough, whose smoke feathers out over the pines. I am sure, were I not a white man, I could not so easily assume its dissipation. The myth of the rugged individual is as real as the region's opioid epidemic: both are addictive, because the long, white winters so badly want self-medication. Both are lethal.

The Measure

Growing up in a family that possessed neither the will nor the finances for distant travel, I was drawn to maps at an early age. New England's dimensions fascinated me. The entire region nearly could fit inside Missouri. Maine was especially intriguing. It was about the size of the other New England states combined, yet it was not even a state in the nation's first decades. The colonial maps in my textbooks always colored it the same shade as Massachusetts, of which it was a province. Some aspect of its identity always appeared parenthetically: Maine (Mass.), or Mass. (Maine). I wondered over the effect of an area being dominated by partially unincorporated territory. How could a state possess an exclave over three times its own size? Wouldn't it make more sense to have regarded Massachusetts as the satellite of Maine? And what of this little world, this New England? What did it mean to imagine community in tidy, regional terms? Here was a *region* so unified as to have its own professional football team. (This greatly confused me; Kansas City Chiefs, Minnesota Vikings—but *New England* Patriots?) I don't recall when I began thinking of myself as a Midwesterner, nor when I began to mark the Dixie inflections of my corner of Missouri. In my education, we did not talk much about the meaning of borders, the scales of empire, or the thumbs on the scales. I cannot recall when I learned which side Missouri took in the Civil War.

Maine is fun to talk about with my elementary-school-aged Missouri nieces and nephews. But they prefer tales of New York City. Projecting my early-life curiosities onto them, I like to share scale. Their aunt and I live in a city that is 300 square miles; Missouri is 69,000 square miles—230 times larger. Our city contains about eight million people; Missouri has about six million people—smaller by 25%. They silently play the numbers, reacting with a mixture of politeness and awe. The youngest has an odd, endearing fascination with the Flatiron Building, always routing conversation back to it, always a little disappointed that it does not figure more prominently into my daily city routines. I had maps at his age. He has architecture.

I am wary of making them poor surveyors. I do not want them to misinterpret, say, the overwhelming visibility of one color on a Presidential election map as a sign of one political party's cultural dominance. The white South has maintained much more than three-fifths of its political authority with this *trompe l'oeil*. But I also want them to reckon with the diminutive size of the nation's culture industry. New York is, in fact, physically small, and quite fragile. 9/11 demonstrated that to my generation. The coronavirus outbreak of 2020 will make it terribly clear to theirs. In any event, I hope my nieces and nephews might see from a more total station. Considering the wholes, they might build resistance to the worst attempts at colonization proceeding from my city and from their own state. Land matters, but land does not vote. Manhattan matters, but it is an island, in space, in history.

New York City fixes itself in memory and imagination. The Maine and Missouri I know were among the first places, inhabited by white people in this country, that capitalism forgot. Both suffered from being arborous and wet. My family came from the Missouri Bootheel, a low-lying region on the Mississippi River, just downstream of its convergence with the Ohio River. In the late nineteenth century, lumber barons harvested the dense cypress groves of the area's mostly uninhabited swampland. Once the "Big Swamp" was cleared of trees, a collusion of land speculators and government agencies turned it into farmland. They dried it out by cutting miles of drainage ditches and levying off portions of the Mississippi. Long nourished by the great river and its local tributaries, the now-unconcealed soil was among the most nutrient-saturated in the world. The Bootheel became a patchwork agricultural region, owned by major landowners, worked by tenant farmers and an African American labor force fairly new to the state. Before the second-wave Great Migration population booms in Kansas City and St. Louis, the Bootheel bore witness to Missouri's peculiar legacy vis-a-vis America's "peculiar institution": it was a former slave state whose black population proportionally increased during Jim Crow. The Bootheel region is presently among the most impoverished in the country.

Maine's deforestation and water misuse go back farther and are better documented; I won't rehearse the stories. But every time I walk through a stand of great eastern white pines, I imagine walking a landscape dominated by those giants, in the days before the British king needed masts for his navy. It must have been the closest thing, in recent history, on the eastern seaboard, to the west's redwood forests. The money is as absent as the old growth. In neither Maine nor Missouri have the people who lived on the most intimate terms with the land profited the most from their use.

When absentee capitalists drain a place to nothing, they generate utopians. The Compromise states have long been the subject and site of social, often religious, idealization. Early European explorers scoured Maine for Norumbega, the fabled golden city of the northeastern Atlantic coast. Joseph Smith was so bold as to locate the garden of Eden outside of present-day Kansas City, and hoped to build a Mormon "New Jerusalem" there, until hostile Missourians, with the "Mormon extermination order" of governor Lilburn Boggs at their back, pushed Smith and his flock out of state. Since the lumber barons, each state has yielded a logjam of social experimenters and prophets. William Dennes Mahan, a Presbyterian minister in Boonville, Missouri, made a splash peddling his *Archko Volume*, which supposedly contained long-lost interviews with people who knew Jesus as a young man. Religious seeker Sarah Farmer drew spiritual leaders from across the globe to teach at her Green Acre Center in Eliot, Maine. The Amish of Seymour and Aroostook. The homestead of Helen and Scott Nearing in Maine. Unity Village in Missouri. Lovejoy.

As I write this, St. Agatha, a village in northern Maine, is working to prevent newcomer/squatter Gary Blankenship from turning the tiny town into the center of what residents feel is his religious cult. In Jackman, Maine, former city manager Tom Kawczynski advocates for the establishment of "The Kingdom of New Albion," a whites-only settlement carved into the state's northern counties. Jackman citizens kick him out. Disgraced televangelist Jim Bakker has set up shop in Branson, Missouri; the state attorney general has sued him for selling a coronavirus "cure" on his broadcasts. Missouri white supremacist Timothy Wilson has been killed in a shootout with the FBI; he was plotting to bomb a Kansas City area hospital. Wilson originally planned to target a synagogue, mosque, or predominantly black school. The coronavirus outbreak, which he blamed on foreigners and his own government, altered his designs. Cape Girardeau County is the birthplace of Terry Jones, the pastor who travelled the country burning Qurans and disseminating anti-Muslim propaganda from 2010 to 2013, setting off a wave of protests in the Middle East. Jones graduated from Cape Central High School in 1969. He was a classmate of Rush Limbaugh.

The two states born of a compromise with people-owners remain the project and projection of the opportunistic, the hopeful, the desperate, the hateful. Chopped up and cut down, they bear cruel cartographies.

The Observer: Spring

Lovejoy Hall is empty and quiet in March 2020. I walk home, down Mayflower Hill on a sunny day. On this route, I sometimes see bald eagles flying over the stream at the base of the hill, perching on the tall pines townside. Today, there are none.

Automobile traffic is reduced to nearly nothing due to the quarantine, but foot traffic is up, so I pass a number of neighborhood walkers. Mainers seem built for social distancing—gladly giving wide berths, happy to wave meekly, happy to just keep walking. It is a friendly introvert's dream.

Were these "my people"? I had not asked that in a while. It is not always a helpful question when you are a peripatetic academic with no privilege of place. Perhaps it occurs to me because historical and cultural affinities cause me to read Maine against the backdrop of my state of birth like no other place I have lived—certainly not New York. Although I find Maine's crabby libertarianism more tolerant of certain kinds of difference than Missouri's more religiously-rooted version, I suspect that, as it would be in Missouri, these Mainers and I would not have much of each other, given sustained contact. Based on political profession, "my people," alas, were as likely to be the Massholes, or the summer folks from Manhattan, whom I crossed in transit on the bookends of the academic calendar.

My states are constituted by compromises written on the backs of people made powerless. I am their beneficiary in many ways. How easy it is to recline into a friendly compromise—how familiar it feels for me, a white man who can play house anywhere and pass well enough. It only requires me, in every case, silencing or forfeiting a few precincts of my identity: a concession of ultimate concerns, a moral blunting. Maine is doing comparatively well in the pandemic. The virus can feel a world away, in the pines. So can George Floyd. How easy for me, if I make the requisite concessions, if I permit the light its dominion, to think of trouble elsewhere. It is deep in my rearing. *The thoughtless, lawless act of a few* . . .

Whether you are an individual or a nation, a compromise may constitute the worst of all options if you are trying to build an integrated life. Unequivocal champions of compromise omit the fact that keeping all members of a whole together is often fatal to the whole, and to the members. If you want to preserve a true union, sometimes you must allow, perhaps enable, some secessions. Of course, those secessions may turn out to be fatal as well. And it is impossible to know for certain when secession is the best choice, when it is mere flight from difference in the service of an idle singularity, less union than monolith. But the dogma of compromise eschews such long-term considerations. It does not reckon with the fact that bills come due. Two hundred years after the Missouri Compromise, a submicroscopic pathogen has delivered a bill. The murder of George Floyd has redelivered another. America is forced to consider the compromised health system of the whole, the compromised immunity of the members, the compromised respiratory system, the compromised morality, all the result of a long series of compromises with immoral powers, that worsen the present national crisis.

Reflecting on Huck Finn's moral and geographic refusals, Azar Nafisi writes, "both the reward and the punishment for his straying from the fold was a permanent state of homelessness." An orphan of Missouri, Huck could brook no compromise. I imagine that mythic river he and Jim commuted, united in the restless chase, in a freedom that would cease at every landing.

Huck learned the price; Jim knew it. That same river runs over the wreck of *The Observer*, down to Lovejoy, empty and quiet. Union and domestic tranquility: they do not come at discounts. You cannot have both.

At the Home

JANUARY PEARSON

My grandmother Livy
curls up on the loveseat

beside Billie,
a woman I don't know.

Both wear pink
terrycloth slippers,

grey elastic pants,
buttonless blouses.

Both have lost their words
along the way,

their sunless arms
entwine, hands clasp—

the aspens in Colorado,
amber leaves wind-swept,

bare branches knobbed
and chilly, two pale

trunks spiral each other,
waiting for snow.

THE TRUTH ABOUT MAMI'S BLOOMERS

HIRAM PEREZ

I am a problem to Miracle from the start. A baby brother means having to grow up faster in a household where growing up fast is already the rule. *Keep the door locked and don't open for strangers.* With that cardinal rule they leave Miracle in charge, even though she only started West Miami Junior High this year, leaving me behind at Coral Terrace where I am in the second grade. Mami and Papi don't have a choice. They both work long hours in factories and other jobs too. Still there is never enough money. The creditors call every day. My sister hides in our room, reading Barbara Cartland novels in bed, so my parents recruit me to translate. We gather around the yellow rotary phone on the kitchen wall, and Mami hands me the receiver. *No, they don't speak English. He says they gave him "lay-off" at the factory. She doesn't know when they can pay.*

"*¿Que dicen? ¿Que dicen?*" Mami asks, awaiting my clumsy translations. Papi chews anxiously on the head of an unlit cigar.

Speaking English feels like a curse sometimes, like when Papi pressures me to bargain with the cashiers at Kmart. It doesn't work that way here, I protest. This isn't Cuba. Mami becomes exasperated. "Why do you have a mouth if you're not going to use it?"

I do not look directly at the cashier: "My father wants to know if you can take a couple of dollars off because he's not working right now." I can barely make eye-contact, anticipating the disdain on the face of the cashier, *una Americana.* When my mother calls me *vergonzoso*, I detect the bitterness in her judgment. Boys should be bold, not shy.

My sister mimics Mami's reproach: "Everything embarrasses him!"

"*¡Sí, hombre!*" my mother exclaims, mistaking my sister's ventriloquism for earnest witness.

My bashfulness is another sign of *mariconería*, even though no one says that word out loud to me. Not until my baby nephew Mayo learns it. Miracle loves that story.

"Remember that time Mayito went around calling everybody a *maricón*, including Mami and Papi and Zuleika and Hugo and everyone laughed like it was the funniest joke ever, and then he called you a *maricón* and they all stopped laughing at the same time? Remember how they told him he could never say that word to you again, ever?"

I remember the confusion and scare in Mayito's eyes. Frozen in my *vergüenza*, I did not know what to do with myself. Poor Mayito thought he was in trouble not realizing I was the true offender.

Some days I am an entertainment to Miracle. Like the time she sees me start for the bathroom and beats me there, stationing herself on the toilet. Knobby knees locked, her skinny legs form an inverted "V." She is as immovable as the Sphynx. My entreaties steel her tenacity. She does not move until I shit in the bathtub. When Mami arrives home from the factory, she screams at us both, but only I feel ashamed. My sister is as shameless as I am shameful.

On cold days during Christmas vacation, I forget her cruelty as we watch *Young and the Restless* huddled under the ownerless faux fur coat that hangs mysteriously in our closet. I love Nikki Reed, the young stripper kidnapped into a cult, but I love her older sister even more, Casey—the responsible med student who always comes to Nikki's rescue. I want us to be like Nikki and Casey.

Miracle resents that I am not required to help with what my mother calls "woman's work." I don't even have to replace the twisty-tie when I grab a slice of bread. Every now and then I volunteer to help my mother with her chores, which hold a strange fascination for me despite their tedium. Mami purses her lips and says *no* angrily, as if "woman's work" will make me a woman—or less *hombre* at least. My sister does not get off so easily. Mami is always after her to help. She complains about how Miracle reads too much, a sure sign of laziness. If you have time to read a book, you have time to mop the floor, she says.

I hear Mami scream at my sister while I watch Saturday morning cartoons. As always, curiosity and my need to feel included get the best of me. I stand in the doorway of our parents' bedroom and watch Miracle fold laundry. Why there is such mystery for me in these mundane chores I do not know. My sister's attention shifts to me and I notice a gleam in her eye. I should know never to trust my sister, especially not when her eyes light up that way, but my naïveté is another mystery.

"Do you want to make Mami laugh?" Miracle asks.

The question intrigues me. We don't ever see Mami laugh.

Miracle grabs a pair of Mami's bloomers and tells me to put them on. "It will make Mami laugh."

At first, I do not know how to respond. I shake my head no. The request confuses me. Can she really be suggesting that I wear bloomers?

"Don't you want to make Mami laugh?" My sister's tone is not accusatory but sad. I am already sensitive to my parents' disillusionment and do not stomach others' disappointment well.

"She's so sad and this will make her laugh."

Her words ensnare me. I take on our mother's hurt and anger as if they are my fault.

"Okay," I relent.

My sister bunches up the bloomers in her hand and rushes me into the bathroom, passing them to me. I remain nervous. Why am I so foolish when it comes to Miracle's schemes? I cannot answer this other than to say that I sense a deep sadness in my sister that is as resolute as her cruelty. Despite her lack of empathy for me, my heart breaks when I glimpse her sorrow. It turns up from behind her eyes when she tells me that Mami and Papi love me better. I want not to disappoint Miracle almost as much as I want to make Mami laugh.

I lock the bathroom door and remove my pants. These bloomers are too sheer, I think. This must be a trap. But it is too late. I commit to my role in Miracle's ruse. After slipping into the bloomers, I open the door warily. The ferocious gleam on her smiling face tells me all I need to know. Immediately I realize my blunder and lock myself in the bathroom. Miracle waits for me to re-emerge. The anger I exaggerate cannot hide the betrayal and humiliation I mostly feel. She threatens to tell our parents that I wore Mami's *blumes*. I imagine this revelation as catastrophic not just for me but for our entire family—worse than anything I've seen on *Young and the Restless*, even Nikki

Reed murdering her father. Miracle offers to keep our secret so long as I do whatever she asks. I don't see any alternative.

The next few weeks I run to and from the kitchen preparing crackers with cream cheese topped with sticky rectangles of guava paste and other snacks for Miracle. The room we share is decorated with her old dolls—dolls she neglected and I coveted. Miracle decides she wants me to feed her dolls as well. I mix a little bit of milk with water and use a tiny baby bottle to pretend to feed her *muñecas*. The spectacle barely entertains her but succeeds in humiliating me. She requires regular pedicures in exchange for her silence and, in no time, I become an expert at removing nail polish with acetone and carefully applying fresh coats of paint.

My indenture lasts several weeks. One day a minor task, delivering a bottle of Malta, pushes me over the edge. I burst into tears en route to our bedroom. My sudden meltdown startles Mami and Papi, usually furious with me when I cry. I tell them everything. They spring up off the velour marigold love seat from where they had been watching *Siempre en Domingo*, the Mexican variety show on channel 23. I don't think I've ever seen them move together so swiftly. Mami calls for Miracle, who emerges from our bedroom. She confesses rather matter-of-factly. I register a moment of astonishment on my parents' faces before the eruption of anger. They become incensed I think not so much by my sister's cruelty as by her emasculation of me, which I abetted. Are they raging at me too when they scream at her?

Papi berates Miracle about her responsibility for her brother, reminding her of our difference in age. Mami's eyes narrow as she repeats "*¿Será posible? ¿Será posible?*" Her lament a grievance to the saints and chorus to Papi's tirade: "Can it be possible? Can it be possible?" Usually, Mami is the explosive one, the figure we fear most, and Papi the peacekeeper. But the infrequency of Papi's fury makes it more terrible. That bellowing voice surely belongs to a stranger, not the affable boat carpenter missing most of his teeth, the man who makes sugary milkshakes out of puffed wheat.

Mami doesn't reach for her *chancleta* this time, and Papi does not demand we place in his hands the *cinturón* that hangs on the doorknob of my parents' bedroom door. The rubber sandal and leather belt are reserved for childish misdeeds; Miracle's offense is too profound for such crude instruments. I shrink inside knowing that the fault lies not with Miracle but with me. In my gut, I know that they scream at Miracle because there is nothing they can do to fix me. I prefer Mami striking me with her *chancleta* to this tension. Wondering if she is frightened, I peek at Miracle. Her insolent expression surprises me. She won't be browbeaten. Her black hair blow-dried and styled into flared sides with a crown of side-swept bangs, she stands her ground like a hero martyring herself to the great injustice of her day.

Stubbornly, she decries my transgression again and again: "But he really did wear Mami's *blumes*."

This line of defense infuriates Mami and Papi even more; it's the one thing they most want not to hear. Their anger at my sister masks a deeper dismay. I really did wear Mami's *blumes*. Miracle remains obstinate. Perhaps she detects the note of panic in their anger.

"*Es la verdad*," she protests sourly. It's the truth.

There is nothing any of us can do about that.

THE SHIT BRANCH

ERICA PLOUFFE LAZURE

Pa had been gone all winter.

It was Christmas night the last time we saw him: the old man in the foyer of our family home, booze-face flushed to red. Mom held a hand to her cheek to contain the sting from his slap.

"Don't tell me what to do," he'd said. Slurred, actually. Something about money. Something about mistletoe. He was in no condition to go anywhere, Mom said. She begged him not to. But of course he was going. Even he knew he'd already pushed beyond what passed for acceptable in the Burns household. There was no other option but out.

Mom knew it. Pa knew it. A bottle of Jameson in his system, and he still knew it. That's how smart he was. We kids knew it, too. But we were too young then to know what words would matter to Pa in a near two-bottle state. To make him stop hitting Mom. To keep him from leaving when a storm was raging. But when he skipped the glass and swilled straight from the bottle, we knew we'd have an early bedtime. But that night, my kid brother Andy showed everyone who was the bravest of us three boys, who was mom's true champion, when he dug out the Monopoly game from the pile under the tree and brought it into the foyer where the folks were having it out. Frankie and I hunched behind the tree as Andy held it, one-handed, like a pizza, a soldier in footie pajamas, and lifted the box between them.

"Hey, guys! Let's play a . . . " he'd said, just as the fake money and hotel shares and Community Chest cards and the little silver-plated goat and automobile and cannon sprawled across the floor.

In the confusion of the cleanup, as everyone fell on hands and knees to pick up the silver-plated trinkets, the fake money, Pa made his exit into the snow-filled dark of the night. We never saw him again.

Andy wailed for days, blamed his tears on the missing racecar. But we all knew better.

Not only had Pa left on Christmas night, he did so in the middle of a Nor'easter blizzard boring down across New England. Pa liked to call these "Yankee Storms" on account of the statewide shutdown, as though snow was a conspiracy. Years later, during a science project for middle school, I learned that Nor'easter storms have a circular quality to how the tiny flakes fall, trapped in a pattern, like a shaken snow globe. For hours that night I stared out my window, watching the tumbling, rolling pattern through the steady streetlight, hoping to see a dark figure barreling home through the world of white.

After Pa left, Mom called the cops, but it took two full days before they did anything about it. And it wasn't until the first big thaw two months later that they found him, stone frozen in a snowdrift, two blocks from our school. We'd pass that snow pile every day, played Fort on it after school, even though none of us felt much like playing. The more time we spent outdoors in the cold meant less time listening to Mom cry. She did little else in that winter-long stretch, the phone extension an arm's length away. When the phone did ring, she'd answer it on the half-ring, and we'd listen at her door, trying to catch from the tone of her voice if Dad was on the other end, or the police. We could always tell if it was police or some business stuff because Mom's voice would shift into some weird pitch that made it sound like she was on TV, like she hadn't spent the past week sobbing in a bathrobe. Other times it was Pa's relatives calling long distance from Carolina, or Pa's former boss at the plant, checking in. We didn't learn until much later that Pa had been fired just before Christmas for drinking on the job.

Amazing where the mind moves in the absence of certainty, how it becomes convinced of the ugliest or strangest from among the available scenarios. After Mom turned out her bedroom light, we three boys would convene by the window in our bedroom, keeping watch, and try to reconstruct what might have happened, what could have happened, and why. I, for one, was convinced we'd get a postcard any day from the Florida Keys.

I'd check the mail, even on Sundays, hoping my theory would prove right, hoping Pa would have written a note just to me, inviting me down there to join him in the sun.

We thought perhaps he'd actually made it down to Hugo's, his favorite bar—although the police reported otherwise.

"Maybe he meant to come back," Andy said, "but he got into a fight with a pack of alien ice bandits."

"I vote for a floozy in a convertible with chains on her tires," Frankie said.

"Maybe he crossed paths with the Abominable Snowman," Andy said.

Looking back it was interesting how convinced Frankie and I were that Pa had up and left. After all, maybe he *was* sick of mom. Sick of us. Sick of the snow. Sick of the mistletoe operation. And our guessing game for his absence made us all look deeper into what was wrong with our family, why someone would choose to leave us in the middle of the biggest storm to hit New England. Meanwhile, the police made no leads. And nothing arrived by mail. And, Mom soon discovered, the mistletoe cash was gone.

When he wasn't drunk, Pa was mostly all right. At dinner, he'd crack jokes about barflies and dumb blondes, midgets who play pianos. He let us take target practice on squirrels and tin cans. Frankie always got the shot, but I faked lousy aim, unwilling to advertise my unwillingness to shoot a squirrel. Sometimes in the summer, while Mom got dinner ready, Pa would pass a can of beer around the living room. We boys would sip at the cold, foamy bubbles and watch the Wheel of Fortune on TV, trying not to wince from the cheap, yeasty tang of Pabst Blue Ribbon. Sometimes Pa would complain about Pat Sajak's haircut. Other times, about the Spanish Pentecostals who held tent meetings in the vacant lot down the street. Or the women's libbers from Brown on their latest march, holding up traffic. Or any Northerner who'd bitch about how hot they were in eighty-degree weather. "Let 'em visit Eastern Carolina," Pa would say. "That'd teach 'em a thing or two about the heat." At Thanksgiving, we'd pile into the car and drive down to see Meemaw in Mewborn. We'd tour the swamps—out to Mattamuskeet or the Great Dismal—to see the ducks in caucus, and keep an eye out for mistletoe in the "sick parts" of the forest.

We'd each be assigned tasks: Track, Shoot, or Catch.

Every year, as we tromped through the woods, armed with shotguns and knives and legions of plastic garbage bags, Pa would tell about mistletoe as though we'd never heard it before.

"The way I know it," Pa said, "we got mistletoe up there because some bird ate one of them white berries from some other tree, and then took a crap in this one." He turned around, his chin craning skyward, and pointed. "And that one, too. Look alive, Track."

"Yes, sir. There, Frankie," I said. "Shoot."

Frankie took aim with the Winchester and missed.

"It ain't no moving target, boy. C'mon," Pa said. "Keep your eye shut. Get it that thing your sight, and get it down here." Frankie shot down a big clump on the third try. Andy—in the role of "Catch"—ran to get it. Pa continued.

"Mistletoe only shows up when the tree's on its way out," Pa would say. "One of the meanest parasites out there."

"Like tapeworm?" Andy asked.

"More of an infestation. Like rats," Pa said. "Get this. The Germans? Call it the 'shit branch'. And we here in America we can't quit kissing beneath it."

I could never shake from my mind the image of some girl kissing a turd on a stick as we hauled our catch out of the woods, Santa-Claus style in plastic trash bags, and into the back of the station wagon. What didn't fit Pa would secure on the roof beneath a bright blue tarp. The next morning, a Saturday, we'd drive north, take turns at rest stops, and Pa would always say, "Guard the shit branch, y'all."

We'd arrive home late Saturday and as soon as dawn hit Sunday morning, all five of us would be up and in operation. We boys would haul the bags of shit branch into the house and empty them, carefully, onto what seemed to be an acre's worth of old sheets that Ma had spread out across the kitchen. Pa would dig out massive spools of fake red velvet ribbon from Woolworth's, and tell us to find our scissors.

"Cut the lengths on an angle about ye long," he said. "Like this. Fold it in half, then snip." While the boys cut the ribbon, Pa would use a Bowie Knife left over from his Korea days to cut the mistletoe into sprigs. Ma tied the bows. Together we made what had to be about a thousand sprigs of mistletoe, and Pa spent the next week roadside, selling off every last one for five dollars apiece. The pair of hand-lettered signs said it all:

Fresh-Caught Mistletoe: $5
Test: free (see attendant)

A few times a week, if my homework was done, I got to tag along with Pa. Turned out, in addition to his sign, Pa had rigged up a sprig that dangled like a line off a fishing pole off the brim of his "Mistletoe Test Hat" and showed it off to every pretty lady who stopped in. Only one took him up on a kiss when I was around, a quick peck on the cheek, and you could tell she was just being nice. Even though everyone says from among the three sons I take after him most, I know Pa probably wasn't the handsomest of men, with his skin cracked in straight lines from nose to jowl, and his thick, paunchy nose. By Christmas Eve, nearly every last one of the sprigs sold, and would Pa give us boys each twenty dollars for our help. It wasn't until I was in college that I understood that mistletoe was the reason why we always had such flush Christmases, and why, after Pa died with two thousand dollars in his wallet, they stopped. Who knew for how long that cash would keep our family afloat?

"Amazing the good money folks'll spend on a chance for a damn kiss," Pa would say. "Happy Shit Branch, son."

Mom wouldn't let us see Dad in his casket. She said it was hard enough to see him in the morgue, his face blackened from frostbite, body mangled from the force of the snowplow. But of course we looked, how could we not, alone at the funeral parlor, Mom talking to the director, surrounded by flowers, waiting for everyone to arrive. Three boys in love with gore? How could we not look?

We looked.

We barely spoke to the people who moved through the reception line. We huddled together at night in the same bed, eyes open and silent. We didn't sleep for a week.

Every once in a while I'll think about that vacant lot, how we three boys had played a full month on that snow pile, defending our territory from imaginary polar bears or ice vampires, as our father lay frozen within. One time, Andy even peed right on it. Just stuck out his wang and tried to write his name in the snow.

"I'm now an official member of the Yellow Snow league," he'd said. We held our noses and complained about the nasal pollution we'd suffered from his piss vapors. Andy gave a sinister laugh, and aimed his wang toward us, and gave it another squirt. Nothing came out.

"Maybe a plow truck hit him," Andy said once, at breakfast, when Mom was downstairs changing the wash. "Maybe he fell down somewhere and they plowed him in."

We dismissed Andy's snowplow theory at the time, along with the Abominable Snowman and Ice Alien gang. But if Dad had been around to hear it, he would have given Andy the Best Guess prize, hands down. Because that's exactly what happened.

When they found him, the inner pockets of Pa's coat were stuffed with objects that could only be described as sentimental: a South of the Border family photo (all of us grinning in fake Mexican hats, mouths shaped into joyous "O's" because the photographer made us all say "taco"); a crushed up piece of mistletoe, with a half-dozen dried-up berries, attached by string to his ballcap; and the ugly-ass Shrinky-Dink Darth Vader keychain that Frankie had made him for Father's Day. And there was the fortune from our last Chinese takeout: "Find humor where you least expect it."

In Pa's clenched hand was the racecar from the damn Monopoly game. And in his wallet, two thousand dollars, cash. That Pa had been trapped dead in a snowdrift this whole time brought an odd relief to everyone, especially to Mom. Sure, he left the house that night mad and drunk with the snow falling and draping in endless frozen ribbons, upending our tiny lives. But at least we knew he wasn't quite ready to quit us. Not yet.

INSTRUCTIONS FOR CHILDREN WHO CONSIDER RUNNING AWAY [51]

NICHOLAS SAMARAS

When the authorities ask you what your name is, say your name is Justice.

Say your name is Living.

Say your name is indigenous to your life.

You are "Child who passes through."

You are "Child who is a tribe of one."

You are "Stands with no more markings."

Say you are returned to the earth. You are whole by yourself.

THE BROWN BODY

HERB HARRIS

Our family colors are beige, mocha, café au lait, and umber. The complexions of my cousins, parents, and grandparents fill every shade of the spectrum between black and white. In our faces, one can see lips that are broad or thin, cheekbones that are high or low, noses that are sharp and aquiline or broad and Nubian. We have hair that may be coarse and tightly curled or silky-straight. It might be blonde, jet-black, or anywhere in between. Our eyes might be deep-set, protuberant, almond-shaped, up- or downturned. Their color might be green, blue, amber, or deep brown. Our physical features mixed and recombined over many generations; we are the children of slavery.

This peculiar institution made every kind of exploitation possible. With little to constrain it, the sexual exploitation of slaves was brutal and widespread. We sometimes build romantic mythologies around figures like Thomas Jefferson to sanitize this history. Mostly, it was just rape. We were coerced into being, and the law made us the property of our lawless fathers. My family conspicuously manifests this aspect of slavery. We differ from other black families only in the variety of features and complexions passed from generation to generation. Our white ancestors would probably not be pleased to see so much of themselves, bearing witness to their misdeeds. Each time I look at myself in the mirror, a host of victims and perpetrators returns my gaze.

What did I expect to learn about this strange heritage by spitting in a tube? I was a reluctant latecomer to the world of DNA-based genealogy. But curiosity overcame my misgivings, and I found myself dropping a DNA sample in the mail. When a few weeks later an email notified me that my results were ready, my hands trembled as I logged in to the 23andMe website. I navigated through the site, which contained many tables, figures, color-coded pie charts, and world maps. I learned that my ancestors had lived in Britain, Ireland, Nigeria, Ghana, Sierra Leone, Spain, and France. It was dizzying to try to imagine all the people and stories behind this list. I read through the numbers that represented the percentages of my ancestry that corresponded to each of these regions. Their significance only gradually sunk in. Although I could not positively identify any of my white ancestors, seventy percent of my heritage came from Europe, and about thirty percent from Africa.

Given my light complexion, I should not have been surprised that I had such a large proportion of European heritage. But I was sure that I had no white ancestors since the times of slavery. My family had lived in a segregated black community for generations. I had always identified as black. Everyone in my family identified as black. How was it possible that more than two-thirds of my ancestry was white? I felt as if every cell in my body contained a foreign substance. Black or white? Which was alien? Which was the host? The proportions of my ancestry are far from the averages of either white- or black-identified populations. In our bell-curve-shaped world, I am a double outlier, impossible to classify.

I have beige skin, loosely curly brown hair, an angular nose, thin lips, and brown almond-shaped eyes. I never know how others read my racially ambiguous appearance. Most of the time, I am mistaken for some ethnic variant of a broadly construed whiteness. The burden generally falls on me to announce that I am a black man. This assertion often evokes looks of confusion and disbelief.

After several hours exploring the DNA-analysis website, my eyes glazed over. I was reading words, but they were not registering. I was randomly clicking links with no idea where I had come from or where I was going. The masses of information before me were not answering my questions. My gaze finally turned away from the screen and came to rest on a collection of family photographs that I kept on my desk.

The oldest of these was a tin Daguerreotype of my grandfather's grandfather—a slave from Virginia named Herbert Harris. I was named after him, but I knew very little about him, and nothing about his parents. His mixed features were evident, even in the grainy image. Beside him was a photograph of my grandfather's other grandfather, Charles Wilder, a slave from South Carolina. I knew nothing about his parents either, but his mixed features were as much in evidence. I had a couple of pictures of my great grandparents, and a picture of my grandfather proudly wearing his World War I uniform. Next to this was my father in his World War II uniform. The lineage continued down to my daughters.

The six generations before me represented frozen moments in a very long history. The photographs were like still frames in a film that had been running for centuries. In every face, I could see some physical manifestation of racial ambiguity. Whether in grainy black-and-white or high-resolution color, the subtle gradations of tones, textures, and features were always apparent. The fugitive images of my family turned race into a continuum that seemed to vanish with time.

But race has not vanished. Its edges have hardened. We have made this illusory concept more real each day. It is a contradiction that inhabits every corner of our society. It is a contradiction that lives inside my body, a sharp blade cleaving one part of myself from another. Race is paradox made flesh.

MATRILINEAL

ARTRESS BETHANY WHITE

I think about a mother tied by blood,
swirling through my body in racial taxonomies,
who will have nothing to do with slave history.

Her love of Disney preferred over historic tableau
technicolor bright with a catchy beat.
I contemplate a mother knotted by blood

I hear tap-tapping through plantation pages
heir to red hair, freckled skin, Scottish genes;
who will have nothing to do with slave history.

Fate is a tale of two ships, African and Euro lineage,
set on a mariner's route, cargo and steerage.
I think about a mother fettered by blood

from childhood our genealogy parsed
to ensure family unity by a woman
wanting nothing to do with slavery.

I have seen the letters and shackled names
the bloated body of words on the sepia page.
I consider this mother tied by blood
whose body has everything to do with slavery.

HANDS

MATHEW GOLDBERG

Esther comes home from the hospital with her arm in a cast. "Wait in the car," she tells Barbara. "He's my husband. I'll get him." With a deep breath, she walks through the front door of the house, then circles the first floor, calling Morris' name. She pauses at the piano and runs the fingers of her unbroken arm along the aged mahogany. Morris had beautiful hands. The hands of a conjurer, she used to think. He played the piano brilliantly, his long, graceful fingers striding across the keys. Esther remembers those fingers tracing her belly before Barbara was born. She strikes a key and cringes as a flat, wobbly note hangs in the air. The piano has not been tuned for a long time.

Morris is in the upstairs bathroom, naked, his hands smeared with shit. "I'm sorry," he tells Esther, holding out his palms. But he apologizes for the wrong thing. This morning he had pushed Esther down the stairs. Falling on her arm hurt, but so did the surprise of the push. More and more, Morris was waking up and not recognizing her. Esther takes Morris' hands and runs them under the sink. She washes one finger at a time, then looks to his shamefully exposed penis. She will bathe him, Esther decides, then dress him in his good suit—the one he had used for piano performances—before they join Barbara in the car. "I'm sorry," Morris repeats. But it's too late. Her daughter has made the proper calls. A room is waiting. It's all worked out.

QUEEN OF HEARTS

DANIELA GARVUE

He dreamed of her, even tried to call. The number had been changed for years. It was a laundromat now. The owner knew his voice.

Hi Don, she said. Still no Joan. Not here.

Tell her I called.

I tell her if I see her.

Okay

Don? You still there?

Yep.

You have a wife? Kids?

Is Joan there?

Maybe she move. Try Facebook.

Don and his wife slept in separate rooms, but he often shuffled in during the morning when she was putting on her leg.

Hi ho, he said.

Ho hum, she replied, always.

I was in Colorado last night.

Oh, lucky. I miss the aspen. I only dreamed of the end of solitaire, when the cards shuffle out.

I remember I worked at NCAR. He pronounced it en-car.

Do you remember the wagon ruts behind the barn? All that paintbrush along Niwot?

I worked with Joan.

That's right.

I'm gonna call her up.

Oh Don.

What's for breakfast.

I'm getting dressed still. You sit quiet and wait.

Hotcakes?

I suppose. If you'll let me up.

If I had a cow that gave such milk, I'd dress her in the finest silk. Ho ho ho, hee hee hee.

Little brown jug how I love thee, Martha said.

That's about rum. I'll have some with my hotcakes.

They laughed gently at each other. Don stood to let Martha push herself out of bed, her small stump dropping into its prosthetic. Smooth white nub like marble.

Ho ho ho, hee hee hee, he said.

Yes, ho hum and so forth, Martha replied, folding her pants over the steel peg.

After breakfast, Don rocked back and forth in his study, turning a name over his tongue. Joan. Joan. Ozone. A hole in the oh Joan. A mole in Joan's zone. Joan done. Jo and one. One Joan. Phone Joan.

'Twas brillig and the slithy toves did gyre and gimble in the wabe.

What was the? These?

The windows rattle. He could be sure of that. They rattle. Had just rattled. But. Had?

Don looked at his book, his chair, with an awareness that accompanies catastrophes and psychedelics. He was reading, and the window had—what? Outgrabe.

Sun spilled through the casement windows onto a small wooden box on the bookshelf. It was dark around the hinges, where rust had aged it. But the top was blonde, auburn along the grain, carved with fine paisley patterns. His hand brushed it; he gasped with recognition of beauty. The light, its clarity. The box. What could it? Had the windows just? She stood outside, looking in through the glass. The sun made red halos in her hair.

Joan.

He stood. The book fell from his lap. He picked it up, set it down. Picked it up, sat in his chair. Ink crawled from the pages.

Hi, Fresh Service Laundry. How can I help you?

Is Joan there?

Um, hold on. [*indistinct*]

Will you tell her I called?

[Give me that.] Don? Hi, this Nancy.

Hi Nancy.

Still no Joan here. How you doing?

Oh, I could complain but I won't.

Good. How your wife?

Martha?

Yah, Martha. She here?

You want to talk to Martha?

Yah. Can you give her the phone?

[Martha?] [Yes?] [Telephone for you.] [Fiddlesticks. *Wheelchair rolling on wood floor.*] Hello?

Hi Martha. My name Nancy. I talk to Don about Joan. You know her?

Joan? Heavens.

He has wrong number. Call every day.

Heavens. [Don, what on earth?]

This a Colorado number. Boulder. Joan lived here before? Martha?

Yes?

Joan lived in Boulder? Before?

Oh, ages ago. We haven't seen her in . . . I'm so sorry, his memory is...

Okay, okay. You have Facebook?

Face—?

Joan have a last name?

Let me see, [Don, what's her last name?] [Who?] [Joan!] [Is that her?] [No, what's her last name?] [Garcia.] Nancy, are you still there?

Yah, I'm here.

It's Garcia.

Okay. Joan Garcia.

[Is that Joan?]

Martha?

Yes.

You okay if I look for her? Maybe I find her number, call you back.

Yes, that would be fine.

Okay. Martha?

Yes?

You take care of Don.

Don and Martha's daughter worked at the university and had summers free. She lived down the road on an acreage she'd bought in the 90s to prove she was not tethered to her parents. They'd bought the hill over her house and moved in several years later. She slept with her phone at full volume, in case either of them needed help at night.

Mom, she called, kicking her boots off at the door. She carried a sieve full of Sungold cherry tomatoes, the last of the season.

In the kitchen.

She looked into her father's study. He held a book to his lap, but stared aside at the window.

Hey dad, she said.

Who's that?

It's me, Carol. Want any tomatoes?

Oh, hi Carol.

They're fresh. See? She shook the sieve at him, but he waved a heavy arm at her. His skin sagged but his bones were still as thick and hard as clubs.

I guess not.

She tucked a strand of hair behind her ear and crept away. Her mother sat in her wheelchair, parked at the kitchen table with a mug of ginger peach tea, flipping through a garden catalogue.

You wouldn't believe the crap they try to sell me, she said. What in the world is a slip and slide?

Well if you'd stop giving them money they might ease off.

Hah. I believe they'd send twice as much out of spite.

Carol sat opposite her mother and offered up her yield. The tomatoes leeched color from the room, seemed to pulse with their own ripeness. Dew on the curves. Little green hats, like rosy elves. And the smell, half spice, half sweet under the ginger peach tea.

This is reality, Carol thought. Over the sieve her mother's face was small and pale. This is reality, and the rest is artificial. What else matters, but growing things?

How did we get so old, Martha thought.

They didn't hear Don lumber past them until he opened the garage door. Keys jingled.

Dad?

Heavens, he's got the keys.

You can't drive.

Then they were around him, Carol taking the keys from his hands and Martha pulling his shirtsleeves.

Oh, get off, I'm going to Colorado. Going to see Joan.

Hello?

Hi Martha. This Nancy. You remember me?

Nancy. Has Don been calling you again?

Yes, but never mind. I like to talk to him. I found her. Joan Garcia.

Really?

Okay, I found her daughter, Eve. Really close. Take care of her mom. Where are they?

Eve live in Boulder. Her mom live in a home in Golden.

A home?

Yah, like a old folk home.

Joan? She can't be more than sixty.

Sixty-five. Still too young for that.

How did you...?

Facebook.

Well, [Martha? What's for dinner?] Just a moment. [What?] [What's for dinner?] [I'm not sure yet.] I'm sorry. He's always hungry these days. Did you talk to Eve?

Me? No, I don't wanna talk to her. I just find her Facebook page. And she has a LinkedIn. So I got her number for you. You got a pen?

[How about a pot pie?] Yes, I have it here. [Four and twenty blackbirds baked in a pie?] [Hush up, Don, I'm on the phone.] Nancy?

Yes.

I'm ready for the number. [Is it Joan?]

Joan had small, hard hands. Always scrabbling at things. Dwarfed by everyday objects. Telephones looked enormous. Books became tomes. He made jokes about how big they made his member look, and Joan would draw her thumb and forefinger close and say, Look at this wee willy, and he'd pretend to be angry and wrestle her to the ground.

Joan in the lab, twirling her glasses around her forefinger. It was a party trick: She folded one temple in against the lens and hooked the other around her finger, spinning until they became a blurry disk, or until they flew across the room.

Joan closing his office door, picking up the article he'd published, flipping to her own name midway through the acknowledgements.

Shouldn't I be first?

Joan at the staff barbecue with her dark-haired child, who beckoned her mother close and opened her pink hands to show her a green beetle. Joan pretending to catch it and eat it, then opening her own hands, giving it back to her daughter. Their matching Cheshire smiles, tiny pointed teeth.

They drifted head-first down a slow river, unable to look forward. Dogs snapped at their heels, snarling from the grass. Willows pooled their tendrils in the shallows where floral patterns rippled just under the surface. Joan's face, marble smooth, staring upward.

Mimsy were the borogroves, she said.

Her cheeks hardened and sank under a violet wave.

Afternoon settled in the house. The refrigerator hummed, rattling the glasses on top. Outside, the fountain burbled into its bowl. Planted at the glass door, the cat watched finches pick at millet along the patio stones. The table sagged under *Better Homes and Gardens*, *Martha Stewart Living*, *Birds & Blooms*, *Modern Homesteading*. Carol popped another tomato into her mouth. It had grown soft and overripe.

What did she say? Eve?

This and that. She remembers Don. She was afraid of him, she said. Remember how he used to sneeze?

Etzch!

Yes! Exactly so. Hardly a toddler then, but she remembers. Also, how he could recite Lewis Carroll until he was blue in the face.

I think he can still do that. Funny what stays and what goes.

Oh, remember how he used to read it to you girls? Of seas and ships and sealing wax, of cabbages and kings.

And why the sea is boiling hot, and whether pigs have wings. Strange to think he recited it to other children.

They were quiet, looking at the last of the oozing cherry tomatoes.

And Joan?

She's in a bad way. On dialysis. Eve thought maybe it would do her some good.

But, don't you feel angry?

Oh Carol, it's too old for anger. Thirty years past? We moved. We put it behind us.

Until now.

Until now.

Martha shifted in her wheelchair, crossed her stump over her good knee. The cat put its soft white paws on her thigh and heaved himself up.

Alright then, you big loaf.

Martha stroked the back of his neck as he kneaded her bladder, purring.

I've made my peace if it's something he feels he has to do.

Back then, Don used to burn brush by the old wagon ruts. Scared Martha to death, watching soft sage embers drift toward the yellow grass. One errant wind and Haystack Mountain would be a pyre. Widows in India, she'd learned, used to throw themselves into their husbands' funeral flames. Marriage is this: burning tinder at the edge of the dry foothills. One lights the flame, the other decides whether to jump in or beat it back.

Southward against the sky, hogback ridges seared pink and gray over Boulder. A spark on their flanks could have been the NCAR building. It passed through the suncatcher Martha was hanging and bored a white hot hole in the cabinet. Don prodded the coals with a long, charred pole.

She set the glass on the counter. The nail was too wide for the hook. Her eyes burned, her throat was thick with soot.

Don, she called, striding out the door.

(How she walked, then! Popping a soft tomato into her mouth, she remembered. How she cut land between her thighs like shears.)

Put it out. Put the damn thing out.

Wind lifted his thin hair, staff in hand like Moses. She took it from him. She stepped into the fire.

Don shouting. Don's great, clumsy arms reaching in, orange. Martha sinking into herself, a small white stone. Don lifting her. The doctors wrapped his arms in white, saying how lucky it was that Martha did not burn. Only the laces of her shoes shriveled into black licorice.

They moved to Nebraska, where Don did not start fires. He piled compost into a black heap and turned its festering belly to dry. There was no barrier between their house and the sky. Martha hung suncatchers in every window.

In the end Carol drove him. Don rode up front, tugging on the seatbelt's shoulder strap.

Christ it's a long drive.

We're not even out of Kearney, dad.

Where the hell are we going?

Colorado. To see Joan.

Oh. Joan. Alright then. When are we going to have lunch?

We'll stop in Ogallala.

I want a roast beef sandwich.

You have that every day. What about a Runza? What about some French fries?

Is it lunch time?

Not yet.

Well. Call me anything you like, but don't call me late for supper.

Carol looked sideways at him, half her mouth pulled in a grin. She had the urge to pull over and put him in the backseat, the way she'd buckled her own children on long drives.

No one would ever make that mistake, she said.

Hell of a drive.

Dad.

Where are we going?

Colorado. Joan.

Alright then.

The road carried them on and on, past cornfields and cottonwoods, into high yellow plains, where grass gave way to sage scrub. They found roast beef sandwiches at Grandma Max's Diner, coffee in Julesburg. Wooden windbreaks caught tumbleweeds along I-76. Semis careened past on their left, and the frightened black snouts of cattle and swine nosed through the sharp gaps.

If I had a cow that gave such milk, I'd dress her in the finest silk.

Carol was quiet. She thought of so many thousands of animals being carried toward abattoirs. Of steel walls and drains in the floor.

Ho ho ho, hee hee hee, little brown jug how I love thee. Don paused, winked at his daughter. That's about rum.

Carol pulled over in Sterling and sobbed in the bathroom. She pulled her father's old address book from her purse and called the laundromat.

Fresh Service Laundry, this Nancy, how can I help you?

Nancy.

Hi, who speaking?

My name is Carol. I'm Don's daughter.

Oh, I shoulda guessed it, you sound just like Martha!

You'll never guess what I'm doing.

You coming here?

That's right.

To Boulder?

We're in Sterling right now. My dad's in the car.

You with him?

I'm in the bathroom.

You better get back there, he can wander away.

He's safe, really.

My dad do that. Old man forget he can't drive. You have the keys with you?

They're right here.

Okay.

Nancy, do you know who Joan was to our family?

I think your mom is a really forgiving lady.

She doesn't have to see her. You know, my dad sang her daughter the same songs as he did to us?

She not his, right?

Oh God. I never thought of that. I don't think so.

What time you getting here?

Another couple of hours. Eve's meeting us in Golden.

Okay. When you done, you come back here. You know Boulder?

I used to live there.

Okay. You come here after. Bring Don. Fresh Service Laundry, by the Goodwill on Canyon.

Alright, I'll come. Nancy?

Someone turned on the air dryer in the bathroom, and Carol let a little choked cry escape into the phone.

It's okay, Carol. I see you soon.

They parked near a squat building with dirty vinyl siding. A row of white vans parked along the curb, Golden Years Retirement Homes printed along their sides. The sun beat heavy on the asphalt, and Don had to shield his eyes from the glittering windshields.

And this was odd because it was the middle of the night.

O Oysters, Don murmured, you've had a pleasant run. Shall we be trotting home again?

Carol shook Eve's hand. She was in her thirties, athletic and competent, the perfect Boulderite. She wore black calf-length leggings and a blue track shirt. Her dark hair was pulled back, flashing silver at the temples. Not beautiful, but striking. Like Joan. Carol looked for hints of her father, but Eve was low and trim with small, sharp teeth and short arms. Carol felt the length of her own limbs, her own blunt incisors, so like Don's.

Look, I'll be honest, Eve said. I don't speak to my mother much. I visit once a week. But I told her you're coming.

Carol nodded.

Hi Don, Eve said, waving through the window. Don lifted a hand in reply. Some of us are out of breath, and all of us are fat, he said.

Eve straightened and smoothed her shirt.

He's got dementia, Carol told her.

That's what Martha said.

Did your mom stay at NCAR?

Eve shrugged. For a while. You know what she was like.

Not really, Carol said.

They both looked at the sky, an impossible Colorado blue.

I try to meditate, Eve said. They say it helps.

Does it?

Sure. But so does keeping my distance. I'll pop my head in with you, but then I'm out of here.

Eve stayed true to her word. She led Carol and Don to a beige hallway on the third floor, where she opened door 3F. A round, pale woman reclined on a mustard yellow couch.

Mom, Eve said, Don's here. She held the door open but did not enter. I'll see you on Sunday, okay?

Sure, sure. Joan waved a small hand, fingers bursting at her rings.

Carol heard Eve's brusque retreat behind her, but she couldn't tear her eyes away from Joan. She was bloated, not plump in a rosy way, but in a drowned way. She wore a riotous shirt of hibiscus blossoms and fern leaves, but neither the shirt nor the bright couch brought any life to her cheeks. Only her roman nose was still hard-edged, focusing the lenses of her half-rim glasses.

Hi Joan.

The older woman propped her hands on her knees and straightened.

Carol. You look just like Martha.

It's…

But it wasn't good to see her at all.

Oh Don, Joan said. You're tall as ever.

Don shuffled forward, stooping under the light fixture. His palms worked together, rubbing over and over the bones of his wrists.

Carol made her escape. Down the elevator, past the lobby desk, to the white-hot row of vans with their blinding glass. Eve had a cigarette in her mouth. She was pulling away, sobbing into a telephone.

Joan on the couch, Joan, pale as the flesh of a turnip. Joan, marble-faced, sinking into a turbid river.

How long? Don wondered. Were the doors always so? Cheap? Didn't he live in a place with light? There was a time when, windows rattling, he looked up. But not here.

You should have seen the other guy, Joan said. She turned her pale face toward his. His arms reached to the fabric of her blouse, to cut away the casing, let the gristle spill out.

She showed him a hard-plastic catheter port above her navel. Her skin was brown and hard around the seal. He remembered the dark hinges of the little wooden box in his study.

Now I don't have to shit or get off the pot, she said, wheezing.

Joan.

Don.

He caught her hand, such a little thing, fingers round and smooth as sausages, the knuckles hardly visible. Squeezing, he felt the hard, ever-digging bones.

Do you still, he asked, spin your glasses?

No. I can't do that anymore.

Do you remember? He moved his thumb and forefinger close. What did you say? Do you remember this?

Joan clapped her palms together. Wee willy, she said. They rocked back and forth on the yellow couch and laughed.

Don wandered into the cafeteria just as Carol was steeling herself to retrieve him.

Ready to go, she said. It wasn't a question.

How about dinner?

We'll have dinner in Boulder.

What about Martha?

She's back in Nebraska. She'll be fine.

Nebraska. Don stared at the linoleum. What the hell does anyone do in Nebraska?

Carol steered him to the car. The sun had relaxed its angle, and the linden trees threw shade over the steering wheel. Highway 93 had changed. The reservoirs and Coal Creek were toothy with subdivisions. Table Mesa and Boulder had crept into the parklands, and now there was no gap between them except NCAR, the enormous research facility at the top of Mesa drive. Pink sandstone towers like battlements rose before the flatirons. They cast long purple shadows over the hill.

Dad, look. You remember this place?

Must be about dinner time, he said. The building flashed out of view, behind a King Soopers.

Fresh Service Laundry was a short brick building with a gray awning on the corner of Folsom and Canyon. The open sign glowed blue and red under the deepening evening. Carol parked by an ancient sedan whose rear window was plastered with the faded sticker: I'm Mad As Hell And I'm Not Going To Take It Anymore!

Dad. Do you want to see Nancy?

Nancy?

The woman you were calling.

Call me anything you like, but don't call me late for supper.

Don't you want to know her? She helped you find Joan.

Don's face drew inward until the flyaways of his brows met over his eyes.

Hadn't we better call Martha?

A woman opened the door and bobbed on her toes. She was short, dressed entirely in red, down to her red sneakers, hair pulled in a black ponytail. It bobbed as she approached the car. Carol rolled down her window.

Hi Carol. Hi Don. She reached into the cab and waved over the steering wheel so vigorously that Carol had to pull back from her jangling bangles. I see the Nebraska plates, I know it's you!

Hi Nancy, Carol and Don said in unison. Carol looked at her father with surprise.

You recognize her?

I guess so.

Of course he recognize me. We talk every day. Don, you find Joan?

Don leaned over his daughter to peer up at the woman outside. She was middle aged, a long gold chain looped three times around her crewneck, thin black brows and eyes, freckles on her smooth cheeks. Clipped speech he knew. He grasped for it like a shell to hold against his ear.

You know Joan.

Sure, I know all about her.

I saw her.

Nancy nodded.

He touched a place just above his navel, feeling for a plastic port.

Age is cruel, he said.

Nancy laughed, flashing thin wire braces. Yah, it is. You know it and I know it.

She leaned forward, balancing her elbows on the window frame, and squeezed Carol's shoulder.

That's a good one, Don. Age is cruel.

Click six of spades to seven of hearts. Drag five of diamonds to its four, freeing up the eight of clubs. Double click, double click, empty the stock pile. Royalty flying upward to their towers, then leaping, defenestrated. Solitaire. A bridge of kings, white and red arches against a billiards-green backdrop, a slinky's track. The queen of hearts jumps next. Then her children, bouncing out of the screen, leaving leaflets behind like time. Memory tells you there is more than one card, but you shuffle back the corners and it's aces all the way down.

Ho hum. Martha stared at the screen.

Martha?

Don stood in the hallway in his blue cotton pajamas, holding the landline to his chest. The yellowed cord curled across his forearms. They were still long and heavy, something brutal about them.

Blunt, she thought, staring at her husband's arms. That's the word.

Summer's light had turned amber and the cottonwoods twitched with fall. The cat stared, but all the finches were gone.

Who was I calling?

I don't know. Nancy?

Nancy?

Oh never mind.

I was about to call someone. But I can't remember.

That's alright. It probably wasn't all that important, then.

Maybe it was the Jabberwocky.

Maybe it was.

The jaws that bite, the claws that catch!

Martha pushed her wheelchair away from the computer. Cards hurled themselves at the screen. She said, And hast thou slain the Jabberwock? Come to my arms, my beamish boy!

Don smiled and dropped the phone to the floor. Oh frabjous day, Callooh! Callay, he said.

He chortled in his joy.

ÁNIMA AQUÁTICA
CAROLYNE WRIGHT

Kingdom of water, watery realm, water
distilled through moss and understory, water

under the tongue, under all the stories—
stories of water, flowing through every tongue

translucencies of water, glimmering through
the forest's clerestories, suffusing sphagnum

and traceries of fern, clerestories lucent as blades
passing through distillation, veins of water,

veins of light, veins of water passing through
the light—spectral lights, spectral dominions,

realms of moss along the under-branches
in all the waverings of water, droplets' domain,

realms of the water-drop, clerestories
reflected in the woodland's Gothic uplift—

High Gothic vaults, groins and buttresses
through which the spectral drops distill

still, venous distillations passing through water,
passing through drops and rivulets, traceries

deepening the grooves, tracing the grooves
into which limestone blocks are fitted,

limestone blocks' repose through centuries of uplift,
centuries of flight pouring through transepts

and along the walls, dissolving and distilling
lime from the crevices, dancing lime out

from the stone, water's glimmering domain,
streaks of moss in crevices, realms of downpour

sluicing through the understory, cataracts
of stone, the high vaults and transepts suffused

with light, capellas and clerestories, buttresses
aloft, praying in all the languages of water

CONTRIBUTOR COMMENTS

Benjamin Bartu, "Celebration"

Benjamin Bartu is an epileptic poet and writer studying Human Rights and Political Reconciliation at Columbia SIPA; he can be found on twitter @alampnamedben.

This poem came on the heels of one of the worst seizures I'd experienced in several years, while traveling in England and feeling quite alone. At that time I felt my brain was trying to end me. I needed that same brain to create something which would give me permission to live. The poem is one of a series I'm writing about epilepsy, all named after disco staples (credit is due here to Kool & The Gang for their song "Celebration").

Christine Boyer, "Second Person"

Christine Boyer's work has been published in So It Goes: the Literary Journal of the Kurt Vonnegut Museum and Library, The Little Patuxent Review, *and others. Find her at christine-boyer.com.*

I wrote "Second Person" when I was grieving the sudden death of my mother. The origins of the essay came from the grief therapy group I attended at the time. There was an interesting phenomenon where people would switch to the second person pronouns—you, yours—when speaking of their own grief. I did it too, and I hadn't realized until I noticed everyone else doing it. Despite the fact that we were all ostensibly there to do the hard work of healing, we still kept distancing ourselves from our grief, which created a sort of limbo.

Jinwoo Chong, "Your Subscription Is Expiring"

Jinwoo Chong is pursuing an MFA at Columbia University. Twitter/Instagram: @jinwoochong

I was interested in the "turn" that occurs three-quarters of the way through this piece. For me, the idea of easing the reader into accepting an original set of conditions, only to then swipe them away and reveal a truth, was an exciting challenge, something I'd always struggled with but admired in other, greater stories. Also, I was once laid off from a magazine, my first job out of college. With these words, I begin to heal.

Leah Dieterich, "What to Do with the Plants"

Leah Dieterich is the author of the memoir Vanishing Twins: A Marriage. *Instagram @andthetidewaswayout Twitter: @leahdieterich*

This piece grew out of a real email I drafted to a friend who was going to water our yard in Los Angeles while we were away, and an affinity I've always had for the tactile qualities of certain plants. It initially was written to be read aloud as part of the Freya Project's reading series, where the prompt was to write about "a time in nature."

Dara Yen Elerath "The Red Hair"

Dara Yen Elerath's debut poetry collection, Dark Braid, *won the John Ciardi Prize for Poetry and is forthcoming in 2020.*

I have an affinity for unreliable or problematic characters; I also love stories that revolve around a single, main image. My attraction to these things relates to a theme I often return to, which is that of obsession. I chose hair as the guiding image for this story because it is charged with certain poetic connotations. My plan was to follow the thoughts of a woman with a particular mania. The red color of the hair eventually emerged as a symbol of something dangerous within her.

Shinelle L. Espaillat, "Water Wars"

Shinelle L. Espaillat currently teaches writing at Dutchess Community College in Poughkeepsie, NY. Find Shinelle at shinelleespaillat.com; @shinelle20 (Twitter); @shinelleespaillat (Instagram).

"Water Wars" began as a way to vent about work. I had worked in spaces where increasingly inconceivable expectations were presented as perfectly acceptable, and in which the hierarchy participated in active, oblivious, trickle-down dehumanization. I had seen multiple work spaces devolve from atmospheres of camaraderie to morale deserts, and the transition could almost always trace back to the installation of a certain kind of leadership: when the people who did the work assumed that the leadership would fail due to blatant incompetence. So, the story evolved to include an exploration of how quickly the absurd becomes the accepted norm.

Joel Fishbane, "mermaid"

Joel Fishbane's novel The Thunder of Giants *is available from St. Martin's Press, while his work has been published in a variety of places, most recently* Ploughshares *and the* New England Review. *joelfishbane.net*

This is part of a story cycle I'm writing about Iris and Gibb that follows their relationship through the years. Most of the stories take place when they're older but I wanted to visit them when they were younger and explore how their relationship began.

Daniela Garvue, "Queen of Hearts"

Daniela Garvue hails from central Nebraska and is currently pursuing an MFA at the University of Montana, where she is a fiction editor at Cutbank Literary Magazine.

This story was inspired by family legend. I grew up on the same acreage as my grandparents, and often stayed with them when I visited home. When my grandfather's memory deteriorated, he tried to pin down his long life into easily digestible fragments, often manifesting as nursery rhymes and simple declaratives. He had a wonderful ear for language, even when he couldn't keep his facts straight. I tried to capture that impression here: memories flashing like the pattern of suits as you shuffle a deck of cards.

Mathew Goldberg, "Hands"

Mathew Goldberg's stories have appeared in The Atlantic, Shenandoah, American Short Fiction, *and* StoryQuarterly, *among others.*

"Hands" was inspired by my grandfather, a Baltimore pianist and band leader. He was born in South Africa after his parents fled Lithuania. My grandfather was in my life, but because of his Alzheimer's, I never fully knew him. Instead, I witnessed his slow mental and physical decline. I wish I'd heard him play piano.

Sandy Brian Hager, "Brody's Letter"

Sandy Brian Hager teaches political economy at City, University of London. Find out more at sbhager.com.

I've never been able to commit to journal writing, but a few years back, as an alternative, I started compiling a list of significant memories from my childhood. My cousin Brody features frequently on that list. I felt compelled to share this particular memory about a letter he wrote to my dad in the form of flash memoir. "Brody's Letter" is a story of childhood innocence and the minor missteps that make it so endearing.

Ryan Harper, "States of Compromise"

Ryan Harper is a visiting assistant professor in Colby College's Department of Religious Studies, where he teaches courses on American religion, the arts, and the environment.

I started working on this essay in early 2019, knowing the Missouri Compromise's 200th anniversary was approaching. Although I originally imagined an entirely-historical article, conditions on the present ground kept throwing me backward and forward in time—reminding me how the United States' compromised present was an inheritance of former concessions. The pandemic hit. Then, George Floyd's murder. Then, the shooting of Jacob Blake. My thoughts became prismatic. The local/national; past/present; Maine/Missouri—in reality, in imagination—I felt I could not consider any one without catching a refracted vision of the others. The essay preserves those dispersions and convergences.

Herb Harris, "The Brown Body"

Herb Harris is a psychiatrist currently working on a memoir. Find him at herbertwharris.com.

I had no idea what to expect when I sent my sample off to 23andMe. The results showed that Britain, Ireland, and northern Europe accounted for about seventy percent of my ancestry. The problem is that I am black. I inherited a light complexion from my slave-owning ancestors, but I grew up in a black family in a segregated neighborhood in a world that defined me as black. These numbers did not change anything, but they became one more part of myself that I struggled to make sense of.

Andrea Jurjević, "*Le Rêve*, Henri Rousseau" and "Pillow Talk with Modigliani's *Kneeling Blue Caryatid*"

Andrea Jurjević is the author of Small Crimes, *winner of the 2015 Philip Levine Poetry Prize, and a translator whose book-length translations from Croatian include* Mamasafari *(Diálogos Press, 2018) and* Dead Letter Office *(The Word Works, 2020).*

I've been writing about the interiority of human life—that place deep within, the infinity mirror of our desires and fears, and how it is such a non-negotiable part of both who we are, and our reality, too. This dark, elemental part of us is our true, core self. Audre Lorde calls it the "woman's place of power." These poems are framed by art. Rousseau's *The Dream* becomes an accidental reflection of reality, and Modigliani's portrait of Anna Akhmatova suggests that perhaps the world is nothing but a dream, an ancient longing.

Erica Plouffe Lazure, "The Shit Branch"

Erica Plouffe Lazure is the author of two flash fiction chapbooks, Sugar Mountain *(2020) and* Heard Around Town *(2015). Her fiction can be found online at https://ericaplouffelazure.com/*

As a former transplant to eastern North Carolina, I dreamed each November of harvesting fresh wild mistletoe and make a killing selling it up North at Christmastime. But I had no ladder. No rifle or knife. Also, I am a terrible tree-climber and it's probably illegal to transport an invasive species across state lines. So instead I built a story around a character with these harvesting skills and tools, who managed, in spite of everything, to demonstrate his (flawed) love for his family through the mistletoe, as told by his son, still pondering the circumstances of his father's death.

Camille Lowry, "I Am Not Still in the Night"

Born in Tanzania, raised in Berkeley, Calif., L.A.- based Camille Lowry has written for Juxtapose Magazine, Swindle Magazine, Huffington Post, *and as a columnist for* Black Voices.

I tend to write about the past, relying on distance to bring vision and wisdom to the work. This piece is one of the few I've written while in the midst of the story. Last summer I was struck by a series of unfortunate injuries. The fall followed with a building frustration that I might never fully heal, and a panic that struck me mentally and physically at night. I was so bewildered by the state I'd landed in, I was driven to write about it, and untangle myself from the story my mind was telling me about my body.

Jo'Van O'Neal, "The Binding"

Jo'Van O'Neal is a Black poet, content creator, and teaching artist currently based in Newburgh, New York. He is a fellow of The Watering Hole and a Hurston/Wright Foundation workshop Alumnus. In 2018, he was an inaugural Open Mouth Readings Writing Retreat participant. His work is forthcoming or featured in Foundry Journal *and* Bayou Magazine.

I've been interrogating my feelings about a lot of things, particularly the relationships I have with the men in my life. And I wanted to articulate to myself the history of those feelings. Not just my own personal history but some of the "history" I was raised into. I think of the patriarchy and I think of violence. Archaic violence, so the biblical telling of the attempted sacrifice of Issac by his father felt like the right place to ground both this poem and my work in progress.

Dayna Patterson, "Self-Portrait as Perdita in 33 Washes of Purple"

Dayna Patterson is the author of Titania in Yellow *(Porkbelly Press, 2019) and* If Mother Braids a Waterfall *(Signature Books, 2020), and she's the founding editor-in-chief of* Psaltery & Lyre. *daynapatterson.com*

In Shakespeare's *The Winter's Tale*, Perdita is abandoned as an infant on the desert shore of Bohemia, exposed and left to die. Perdita's mother is pronounced dead after the shock of losing her son and infant Perdita. In my own tale, my mother suffered from debilitating postpartum depression after having three babies in three years. Numb, she left my father and didn't resurface in my life until about a decade later. My mother and I have made peace, and that peace is spacious enough to face ache; it dares to ponder "if."

January Pearson, "At the Home"

January Pearson lives in Southern California and teaches in the English department at Purdue Global University.

When we visited our grandmother, my husband and I were anxious about seeing her, knowing that her dementia had progressed considerably. But when we arrived and saw her smiling like a child, cuddled up next to Billie on that worn couch, we were comforted. I was struck by the beauty of their innocent affection, how openly they clung to one another, as though they would never let go.

Hiram Perez, "The Truth About Mami's Bloomers"

Hiram Perez (he/him) is an Associate Professor of English at Vassar College, where he also currently serves as the Director of the Women's Studies Program.

As an academic, I have struggled to write about shame. The turn to memoir allowed me to linger more satisfyingly on the contradictions of shame. My difficult childhood relationship with my older sister, related in "The Truth About Mami's Bloomers," provides a deep source of ambivalence. Memoir allowed me to ruminate on my childhood identification with my sister without demanding a resolution from the contradiction of her cruelty and my attachment to her.

R. R. Pinto, "The Girl Who Cried Flowers"

R. R. Pinto holds a B.A. in English from William & Mary. She lives and works in Virginia with her family, two dogs, and a struggling orchid.

I spent a lot of time at home this year, and was able to pay attention to what was in front of me. I watched as the flowers in my yard took turns growing tall and peaking in color—yellow, pink, and blue. I watched as they dropped their seeds. I remembered how I used to draw them, a long time ago. I remembered why I stopped. I watched as my daughter watered them. I watched her draw a sign, "BLM," written large. And then I watched as she marched, sign held high. Humbled, I unfroze and wrote this piece.

Nicholas Samaras, "Instructions for Children Who Consider Running Away [51]"

Nicholas Samaras is from Patmos, Greece (the "Island of the Apocalypse"), and at the time of the political Greek Junta Military Dictatorship ("Coup of the Generals") was brought in exile to be raised further in America. After having lived in Greece, Asia Minor, England, Wales, Belgium, Switzerland, Italy, Austria, Germany, Yugoslavia, Jerusalem, thirteen states in America, he now writes from a place of permanent exile. His first book, Hands of the Saddlemaker, *won* The Yale Series of Younger Poets Award. *His next book,* American Psalm, World Psalm, *came out from Ashland Poetry Press (2014).*

Photo credit: Karen Paluso

My biological parent found the perfect place to hide underground: the American Military—through which he was able to avoid confrontation. When an issue arose, he "put in" for a transfer and shipped out to another Military base in another country, hauling his captive family with him, and the beatings he inflicted. At fourteen, I vowed, if they placed a man on the moon, I would take the giant step and run away. On June 21st, 1969, with a man on the moon, I stepped off the mountain radar site we lived on, and went missing for two months.

Derek Sheffield, "Middle School" and "A Response to a Pair of Forest Plots"

Read more about Derek at dereksheffield.com.

Twitter: @Terrainorg

Both of these poems are in response to beautiful wilds I have been fortunate enough to be in the presence of. In one case, by being a visiting writer at the H.J. Andrews Experimental Forest in Blue River, Oregon, courtesy of the Spring Creek Project; and in the other, by being the father of an incredibly creative and expressive daughter who seems to never stop growing and changing into a form, a person, a force quite beyond me.

Artress Bethany White, "Matrilineal"

Artress Bethany White—poet, essayist, and literary critic—is the author of poetry collections Fast Fat Girls in Pink Hot Pants *(2012) and* My Afmerica *(Trio House Press, 2019), and the essay collection* Survivior's Guilt: Essays on Race and American Identity *(New Rivers Press, 2020). Read more at artressbethanywhite.com.*

It is a miracle that this poem exists at all. My mother was the bearer of an oral slave narrative passed down to her by her mother, who inherited it from her father, who was born on a plantation in 1865. Dutifully, she passed it down to me. This story, however, is as much as she ever wanted to share about slavery. She did not watch *Roots*: too sad. She would not discuss the particulars of slavery from concubinage to physical torture as discipline: too painful. As a scholar, I wanted to document this critical multiracial family history, and the narrative of only being four generations removed from American institutionalized enslavement.

Carolyne Wright, "Ánima Aquática"

Carolyne Wright's latest book is This Dream the World: New & Selected Poems *(Lost Horse Press, 2017). She has 16 earlier books and anthologies of poetry, essays, and translation, and has received a 2020-2021 Fulbright Scholar Award to Bahia, Brazil. carolynewright.wordpress.com. Facebook: Carolyne Lee Wright*

Photo credit: Sherwin Eng courtesy of the Jack Straw Cultural Center

This poem emerged from a workshop by Seattle-based Chilean poet Eugenia Toledo several years ago for Hugo House's Write-O-Rama. Eugenia read in Spanish a poem called "*Ánima*" by Cuban poet José Kozer, and we all wrote responses. Kozer's poem had one line about water:"El único recurso del agua que corre." Propelled by the rhythms and musicality of Eugenia's reading, I found myself improvising on water, tracing the movements of water in the temperate rainforests of my native Pacific Northwest. The poem became a litany, constructing in imagery a Gothic cathedral of water in the groves of this mental rainforest.